BROWN GIRL DREAMING

brown girl dreaming

JACQUELINE
WOODSON

THORNDIKE PRESS

A part of Gale, a Cengage Company

GALE
A Cengage Company

Farmington Hills, Mich • San Francisco • New York • Waterville, Maine
Meriden, Conn • Mason, Ohio • Chicago

Recommended for Middle Readers.
Copyright © 2017 by Jacqueline Woodson.
"Dreams," and "Poem [2]" from THE COLLECTED POEMS OF LANGSTON HUGHES by Langston Hughes, edited by Arnold Rampersad with David Roessel, Associate Editor, copyright © 1994 by the Estate of Langston Hughes.
Used by permission of Alfred A. Knopf, an imprint of the Knopf Doubleday Publishing Group, a division of Random House LLC. All rights reserved.
Used by permission of Harold Ober Associates Incorporated.
"Twistin' the Night Away" written by Sam Cooke. Published by ABKCO Music, Inc. Used by permission. All rights reserved.
Thorndike Press, a part of Gale, a Cengage Company.

ALL RIGHTS RESERVED
Thorndike Press® Large Print The Literacy Bridge.
The text of this Large Print edition is unabridged.
Other aspects of the book may vary from the original edition.
Set in 16 pt. Plantin.

LIBRARY OF CONGRESS CATALOGING-IN-PUBLICATION DATA

Names: Woodson, Jacqueline, author.
Title: Brown girl dreaming / by Jacqueline Woodson.
Description: Large print edition. | Waterville, Maine : Thorndike Press, a part of Gale, a Cengage Company, 2017. | Series: Thorndike Press large print the literacy bridge
Identifiers: LCCN 2017024042| ISBN 9781432843151 (hardcover) | ISBN 143284315X (hardcover)
Subjects: LCSH: Woodson, Jacqueline—Poetry. | Authors, American—20th century—Biography—Poetry. | African American women authors—Biography—Poetry. | Large type books. | BISAC: JUVENILE NONFICTION / Biography & Autobiography / Literary. | JUVENILE NONFICTION / Biography & Autobiography / Women. | JUVENILE NONFICTION / Social Issues / Prejudice & Racism.
Classification: LCC PS3573.O64524 Z46 2017 | DDC 811/.54 [B]—dc23
LC record available at https://lccn.loc.gov/2017024042

Published in 2017 by arrangement with Nancy Paulsen Books, an imprint of Penguin Young Readers Group, a division of Penguin Random House LLC

Printed in Mexico
7 8 9 10 11 12 23 22 21 20 19

This book is for my family —
past, present and future.
With love.

CONTENTS

FAMILY TREE 8

PART I. I AM BORN 13

PART II. THE STORIES OF SOUTH
CAROLINA RUN LIKE RIVERS . . . 59

PART III. FOLLOWED THE SKY'S
MIRRORED CONSTELLATION TO
FREEDOM 171

PART IV. DEEP IN MY HEART, I DO
BELIEVE 249

PART V. READY TO CHANGE THE
WORLD 345

AUTHOR'S NOTE. 391
THANKFULS 395
FAMILY PHOTOS 398

7

WOODSON FAMILY TREE

Hope Austin ——— ⊗ ——— Grace Vivian
Woodson   Whitfield Woodson
1906-1978   1916-1988

Cornelia Ann   Ada   Alicia Ruth
Woodson Long   Woodson   Woodson
1936-2005   1939   1948

Edward   David Arthur
Woodson   (Woody) Woodson
1939-1939   1940-2014

Jack Austin
Woodson
1937

Hope Austin   Odella Caroline
Woodson   Woodson
1960   1961

IRBY FAMILY TREE

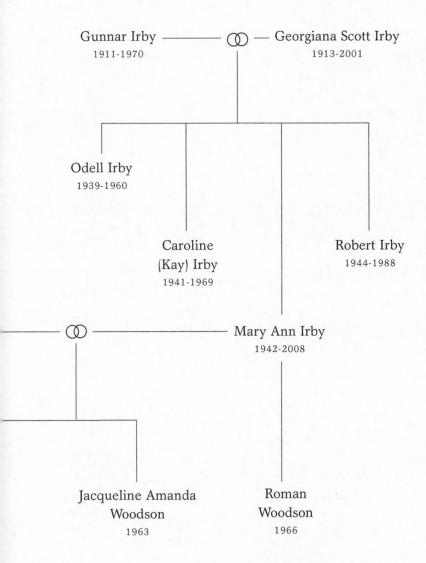

Gunnar Irby ——————— ⊙⊙ — Georgiana Scott Irby
1911-1970   1913-2001

Odell Irby
1939-1960

Caroline
(Kay) Irby
1941-1969

Robert Irby
1944-1988

—— ⊙⊙ ———————————— Mary Ann Irby
1942-2008

Jacqueline Amanda
Woodson
1963

Roman
Woodson
1966

Hold fast to dreams
For if dreams die
Life is a broken-winged bird
That cannot fly.

Hold fast to dreams
For when dreams go
Life is a barren field
Frozen with snow.
— Langston Hughes

PART I

i am born

FEBRUARY 12, 1963

I am born on a Tuesday at University
  Hospital
Columbus, Ohio,
USA —
a country caught

between Black and White.

I am born not long from the time
or far from the place
where
my great-great-grandparents
worked the deep rich land
unfree
dawn till dusk
unpaid
drank cool water from scooped-out gourds
looked up and followed
the sky's mirrored constellation
to freedom.

I am born as the South explodes,
too many people too many years

enslaved, then emancipated
but not free, the people
who look like me
keep fighting
and marching
and getting killed
so that today —
February 12, 1963
and every day from this moment on,
brown children like me can grow up
free. Can grow up
learning and voting and walking and riding
wherever *we* want.

I am born in Ohio but
the stories of South Carolina already run
like rivers
through my veins.

Second Daughter's
Second Day on Earth

My birth certificate says: Female Negro
Mother: Mary Anne Irby, 22, Negro
Father: Jack Austin Woodson, 25, Negro

In Birmingham, Alabama, Martin Luther
  King Jr.
  is planning a march on Washington,
  where
John F. Kennedy is president.
In Harlem, Malcolm X is standing on a
  soapbox
  talking about a revolution.

Outside the window of University Hospital,
snow is slowly falling. So much already
covers this vast Ohio ground.

In Montgomery, only seven years have
  passed
  since Rosa Parks refused
to give up

her seat on a city bus.

I am born brown-skinned, black-haired
and wide-eyed.
I am born Negro here and Colored there

and somewhere else,
the Freedom Singers have linked arms,
their protests rising into song:
Deep in my heart, I do believe
that we shall overcome someday.

and somewhere else, James Baldwin
is writing about injustice, each novel,
each essay, changing the world.

I do not yet know who I'll be
what I'll say
how I'll say it . . .

Not even three years have passed since a
   brown girl
named Ruby Bridges
walked into an all-white school.
Armed guards surrounded her while
   hundreds
of white people spat and called her names.

She was six years old.

I do not know if I'll be strong like Ruby.

I do not know what the world will look like
when I am finally able to walk, speak,
write . . .
Another Buckeye!
the nurse says to my mother.
Already, I am being named for this place.
Ohio. The Buckeye State.
My fingers curl into fists, automatically
This is the way, *my mother said,*
of every baby's hand.
I do not know if these hands will become
Malcolm's — raised and fisted
or Martin's — open and asking
or James's — curled around a pen.
I do not know if these hands will be
Rosa's
or Ruby's
gently gloved
and fiercely folded
calmly in a lap,
on a desk,
around a book,
ready
to change the world . . .

A Girl Named Jack

Good enough name for me, my father said
the day I was born.
*Don't see why
she can't have it, too.*

But the women said no.
My mother first.
Then each aunt, pulling my pink blanket
    back
patting the crop of thick curls
tugging at my new toes
touching my cheeks.

We won't have a girl named Jack, my
    mother said.

And my father's sisters whispered,
A boy named Jack was bad enough.
But only so my mother could hear.
Name a girl Jack, my father said,
and she can't help but

grow up strong.
Raise her right, my father said,
and she'll make that name her own.

Name a girl Jack
and people will look at her twice, my father
said.

For no good reason but to ask if her parents
were crazy, my mother said.

And back and forth it went until I was
Jackie
and my father left the hospital mad.

My mother said to my aunts,
Hand me that pen, wrote
Jacqueline where it asked for a name.
Jacqueline, just in case
someone thought to drop the *ie.*

Jacqueline, just in case
I grew up and wanted something a little bit
longer
and further away from
Jack.

THE WOODSONS OF OHIO

My father's family
can trace their history back
to Thomas Woodson of Chillicothe, said to
  be
the first son
of Thomas Jefferson and Sally Hemings
some say
this isn't so but . . .

the Woodsons of Ohio know
what the Woodsons coming before them
left behind, in Bibles, in stories,
in history coming down through time

so

ask any Woodson why
you can't go down the Woodson line
without
finding
doctors and lawyers and teachers

22

athletes and scholars and people in
   government
they'll say,

We had a head start.
They'll say,
Thomas Woodson expected the best of us.
They'll lean back, lace their fingers
across their chests,
smile a smile that's older than time, say,

*Well it all started back before Thomas
   Jefferson*
Woodson of Chillicothe . . .

and they'll begin to tell our long, long
   story.

THE GHOSTS OF THE NELSONVILLE HOUSE

The Woodsons are one
of the few Black families in this town, their
  house
is big and white and sits
on a hill.

Look up
to see them
through the high windows
inside a kitchen filled with the light
of a watery Nelsonville sun. In the parlor
a fireplace burns warmth
into the long Ohio winter.

Keep looking and it's spring again,
the light's gold now, and dancing
across the pine floors.

Once, there were so many children here
running through this house
up and down the stairs, hiding under beds

24

and in trunks,

sneaking into the kitchen for tiny pieces
of icebox cake, cold fried chicken,
thick slices of their mother's honey ham . . .

Once, my father was a baby here
and then he was a boy . . .

But that was a long time ago.

In the photos my grandfather is taller than
   everybody
and my grandmother just an inch smaller.

On the walls their children run through
   fields,
      play in pools,
dance in teen-filled rooms, all of them

grown up and gone now —
but wait!

Look closely:

There's Aunt Alicia, the baby girl,
curls spiraling over her shoulders, her
   hands
cupped around a bouquet of flowers. Only
four years old in that picture, and already,

a reader.

Beside Alicia another picture, my father,
  Jack,
the oldest boy.
Eight years old and mad about something
or is it someone
we cannot see?

In another picture, my uncle Woody,
baby boy
laughing and pointing
the Nelsonville house behind him and
  maybe
his brother at the end of his pointed finger.

My aunt Anne in her nurse's uniform,
my aunt Ada in her university sweater
Buckeye to the bone . . .

The children of Hope and Grace.

Look closely. There I am
in the furrow of Jack's brow,
in the slyness of Alicia's smile,
in the bend of Grace's hand . . .

There I am . . .

Beginning.

IT'LL BE SCARY SOMETIMES

My great-great-grandfather on my father's
  side
was born free in Ohio,

1832.

Built his home and farmed his land,
then dug for coal when the farming
wasn't enough. Fought hard
in the war. His name in stone now
on the Civil War Memorial:

William J. Woodson
United States Colored Troops,
Union, Company B 5th Regt.

A long time dead but living still
among the other soldiers
on that monument in Washington, D.C.

His son was sent to Nelsonville

27

lived with an aunt

William Woodson
the only brown boy in an all-white school.

You'll face this in your life someday,
my mother will tell us
over and over again.
A moment when you walk into a room and

no one there is like you.

It'll be scary sometimes. But think of William
  Woodson
and you'll be all right.

28

FOOTBALL DREAMS

No one was faster
than my father on the football field.
No one could keep him
from crossing the line. Then
touching down again.
Coaches were watching the way he moved,
his easy stride, his long arms reaching
up, snatching the ball from its soft pocket
of air.

My father dreamed football dreams,
and woke to a scholarship
at Ohio State University.
Grown now
living the big-city life
in Columbus
just sixty miles
from Nelsonville
and from there
Interstate 70 could get you
on your way west to Chicago

29

Interstate 77 could take you south
but my father said
no colored Buckeye in his right mind
would ever want to go there.

From Columbus, my father said,
you could go just about
anywhere.

OTHER PEOPLE'S MEMORY

You were born in the morning, Grandma
  Georgiana said.
I remember the sound of the birds. Mean
old blue jays squawking. They like to fight,
  you know.
Don't mess with blue jays!
I hear they can kill a cat if they get mad
  enough.

And then the phone was ringing.
Through all that static and squawking, I
  heard
your mama telling me you'd come.
Another girl, I stood there thinking,
so close to the first one.
Just like your mama and Caroline. Not even
a year between them and so close, you could
  hardly tell
where one ended and the other started.
And that's how I know you came in the
  morning.

That's how I remember.

You came in the late afternoon, my mother
    said.
Two days after I turned twenty-two.
Your father was at work.
Took a rush hour bus
trying
to get to you. But
by the time he arrived,
you were already here.
He missed the moment, my mother said,
but what else is new.

You're the one that was born near night,
    my father says.
When I saw you, I said, She's the unlucky
    one
come out looking just like her daddy.
He laughs. *Right off the bat, I told your*
    mama,
We're gonna call this one after me.

My time of birth wasn't listed
on the certificate, then got lost again
amid other people's bad memory.

No Returns

When my mother comes home
from the hospital with me,
my older brother takes one look
inside the pink blanket, says,
Take her back. We already have one of
   those.

Already three years old and still doesn't
   understand
how something so tiny and new
can't be returned.

How to Listen #1

Somewhere in my brain
each laugh, tear and lullaby
becomes *memory.*

UNCLE ODELL

Six months before my big sister is born,
my uncle Odell is hit by a car
while home in South Carolina
on leave from the Navy.

When the phone rang in the Nelsonville
  house,
maybe my mother was out hanging laundry
on the line or down in the kitchen
speaking softly with her mother-in-law,
  Grace, missing
her own mama back home.
Maybe the car was packed and ready for
  the drive
back to Columbus — the place my father
called the Big City — now *their* home.
But every Saturday morning, they drove
the hour to Nelsonville and stayed
till Sunday night.

Maybe right before the phone rang,

tomorrow

was just another day.

But when the news of my uncle's dying
traveled from the place he fell in South
    Carolina,
to the cold March morning in Ohio,
my mother looked out into a gray day
that would change her forever.

Your brother

my mother heard her own mother say
and then there was only a roaring in the air
    around her
a new pain where once there wasn't pain
a hollowness where only minutes before
she had been whole.

GOOD NEWS

Months before the bone-cold
Buckeye winter settles over Ohio,
the last September light brings

my older sister,

named
Odella Caroline after my uncle Odell
and my aunt Caroline.

In South Carolina, the phone rings.

As my mother's mother moves toward it,
she closes her eyes,
then opens them to look out over her yard.
As she reaches for it,
she watches the way the light slips through
the heavy pine needles, dapples everything
with sweet September light . . .

Her hand on the phone now, she lifts it

praying silently
for the good news
the sweet chill of autumn
is finally bringing her way.

MY MOTHER AND GRACE

It is the South that brings my mother
and my father's mother, Grace,
together.
Grace's family is from Greenville, too.
So my mother
is home to her, in a way her own kids
can't understand.
You know how those Woodsons are, Grace
says.
The Woodsons this and the North that
making Mama smile, remember
that Grace, too, was someone else before.
Remember
that Grace, like my mother, wasn't always a
Woodson.

They are *home* to each other, Grace
to my mother is as familiar
as the Greenville air.

Both know that southern way of talking

without words, remember when
the heat of summer
could melt the mouth,
so southerners stayed quiet
looked out over the land,
nodded at what seemed like nothing
but that silent nod said everything
anyone needed to hear.

Here in Ohio, my mother and Grace
aren't afraid
of too much air between words, are happy
just for another familiar body in the room.

But the few words in my mother's mouth
become the *missing*
after Odell dies — a different silence
than either of them has ever known.

I'm sorry about your brother, Grace says.
*Guess God needed him back and sent you a
    baby girl.*
But both of them know
the hole that is the missing isn't filled now.
Uhmm, my mother says.
Bless the dead and the living, Grace says.
Then more silence
both of them knowing
there's nothing left to say.

EACH WINTER

Each winter
just as the first of the snow begins to fall,
my mother goes home to South Carolina.

Sometimes,

my father goes with her but mostly,
he doesn't.

So she gets on the bus alone.
The first year with one,
the second year with two,
and finally with three children, Hope and
  Dell hugging
each leg and me
in her arms. Always
there is a fight before she leaves.

Ohio

is where my father wants to be

but to my mother
Ohio will never be home,
no matter
how many plants she brings
indoors each winter, singing softly to them,
the lilt of her words a breath
of warm air moving over each leaf.
In return, they hold on to their color
even as the snow begins to fall. A reminder
of the deep green South. A promise
of life

somewhere.

JOURNEY

You can keep your South, my father says.
The way they treated us down there,
I got your mama out as quick as I could.
Brought her right up here to Ohio.

Told her there's never gonna be a Woodson
that sits in the back of the bus.
Never gonna be a Woodson that has to
Yes sir and No sir white people.
Never gonna be a Woodson made to look
  down
at the ground.

All you kids are stronger than that, my father
  says.
All you Woodson kids deserve to be
as good as you already are.

Yes sirree, Bob, my father says.
You can keep your South Carolina.

GREENVILLE,
SOUTH CAROLINA, 1963

On the bus, my mother moves with us to
   the back.
It is 1963
in South Carolina.
Too dangerous to sit closer to the front
   and dare the driver
to make her move. Not with us. Not now.
Me in her arms all of three months old.
   My sister and brother squeezed into the
   seat beside her. White shirt, tie, and my
   brother's head shaved clean.
   My sister's braids
white ribboned.

Sit up straight, my mother says.
She tells my brother to take his fingers
   out of his mouth.
They do what is asked of them.
Although they don't know why they have
   to.
This isn't Ohio, my mother says,

as though we understand.
Her mouth a small lipsticked dash, her
  back
sharp as a line. DO NOT CROSS!
COLOREDS TO THE BACK!
Step off the curb if a white person comes
  toward you
don't look them in the eye. Yes sir. No sir.
  My apologies.
Her eyes straight ahead, my mother
is miles away from here.

Then her mouth softens, her hand moves
  gently
over my brother's warm head. He is three
  years old,
his wide eyes open to the world, his too-big
  ears
already listening. *We're as good as anybody,*
my mother whispers.

As good as anybody.

HOME

Soon . . .

We are near my other grandparents' house,
  small red stone,
immense yard surrounding it.
Hall Street.
A front porch swing thirsty for oil.
A pot of azaleas blooming.
A pine tree.
Red dirt wafting up
around my mother's newly polished shoes.

Welcome home, my grandparents say.
  Their warm brown
arms around us. A white handkerchief,
  embroidered with blue
to wipe away my mother's tears. And me,
the new baby, set deep
inside this love.

THE COUSINS

It's my mother's birthday and the music
is turned up loud.

Her cousins all around her — the way it
   was
   before she left.
The same cousins she played with as a girl.
Remember the time, they ask,

When we stole Miz Carter's peach pie off her
   windowsill,
got stuck in that ditch down below Todd's
   house,
climbed that fence and snuck into Greenville
   pool,
weren't scared about getting arrested either,
   shoot!
nobody telling us where we can and can't
   swim!

And she laughs, remembering it all.

On the radio, Sam Cooke is singing
  "Twistin' the Night Away":

> *Let me tell you 'bout a place*
> *Somewhere up-a New York way*

The cousins have come from as far away as
  Spartanburg
the boys dressed in skinny-legged pants,
the girls in flowy skirts that swirl out, when
  they spin
twisting the night away.
Cousin Dorothy's fiancé, holding tight to
  her hand
  as they twist
Cousin Sam dancing with Mama, ready to
  catch her
  if she falls, he says
and my mother remembers being a little
  girl,
  looking down
scared from a high-up tree
and seeing her cousin there — waiting.

> *Here they have a lot of fun*
> *Puttin' trouble on the run*
> *Twistin' the night away.*

I knew you weren't staying up North, the
  cousins say.

You belong here with us.
My mother throws her head back,
  her newly pressed and curled hair
  gleaming
her smile the same one she had
  before she left for Columbus.
She's MaryAnn Irby again. Georgiana and
  Gunnar's
  youngest daughter.

She's home.

NIGHT BUS

My father arrives on a night bus, his hat in
   his hands.
It is May now and the rain is coming
   down.
   Later with the end of this rain
will come the sweet smell of honeysuckle
   but for now,
there is only the sky opening and my
   father's tears.
I'm sorry, he whispers.

This fight is over for now.

Tomorrow, we will travel as a family
back to Columbus, Ohio,
Hope and Dell fighting for a place
on my father's lap. Greenville
with its separate ways growing small
behind us.

For now, my parents stand hugging

in the warm Carolina rain.

No past.

No future.

Just this perfect Now.

AFTER GREENVILLE #1

After the chicken is fried and wrapped in
  wax paper,
tucked gently into cardboard shoe boxes
  and tied with string . . .

After the corn bread is cut into wedges, the
  peaches
washed and dried . . .

After the sweet tea is poured into mason
  jars twisted tight
and the deviled eggs are scooped back
  inside their egg-white beds
slipped into porcelain bowls that are my
  mother's now,
  a gift
her mother sends with her on the
  journey . . .

After the clothes are folded back into
  suitcases,

the hair ribbons and shirts washed and
  ironed . . .

After my mother's lipstick is on and my
  father's
scratchy beginnings of a beard are
  gone . . .

After our faces are coated
with a thin layer of Vaseline gently wiped
  off again
with a cool, wet cloth . . .

then it is time to say our good-byes,
  the small clutch of us children
pressed against my grandmother's apron,
  her tears
quickly blinked away . . .

After the night falls and it is safe
  for brown people to leave
the South without getting stopped
and sometimes beaten
and always questioned:

Are you one of those Freedom Riders?
Are you one of those Civil Rights People?
What gives you the right . . . ?

We board the Greyhound bus, bound
for Ohio.

RIVERS

The Hocking River moves like a flowing
  arm away
from the Ohio River
runs through towns as though
it's chasing its own freedom, the same way
the Ohio runs north from Virginia until
it's safely away
from the South.

Each town the Hocking touches tells a
  story:
Athens
Coolville
Lancaster
Nelsonville,
each
waits for the Hocking water to wash
  through. Then

as though the river remembers where it
  belongs

and what it belongs to,
it circles back, joins up with
    the Ohio again
    as if to say,

I'm sorry.
    as if to say,
I went away from here
but now
    I'm home again.

Leaving Columbus

When my parents fight for the final time,
my older brother is four,
my sister is nearly three,
and I have just celebrated my first birthday

without celebration.

There is only one photograph of them
  from their time together
a wedding picture, torn from a local
  newspaper
him in a suit and tie,
her in a bride gown, beautiful
although neither one
is smiling.

Only one photograph.

Maybe the memory of Columbus was too
  much
for my mother to save

anymore.
Maybe the memory of my mother
was a painful stone inside my father's
   heart.
But what did it look like
when she finally left him?

A woman nearly six feet tall,
   straight-backed
and proud, heading down
a cold Columbus street, two small children
beside her and a still-crawling baby
in her arms.

My father, whose reddish-brown skin
would later remind me
of the red dirt of the South
and all that was rich about it, standing
in the yard, one hand
on the black metal railing, the other lifting
into a weak wave good-bye.

As though we were simply guests
leaving Sunday supper.

the
stories
of
south carolina
run
like rivers

OUR NAMES

In South Carolina, we become
The Grandchildren
Gunnar's Three Little Ones
Sister Irby's Grands
MaryAnn's Babies

And when we are called by our names
my grandmother
makes them all one
HopeDellJackie
but my grandfather
takes his sweet time, saying each
as if he has all day long

or a whole lifetime.

OHIO BEHIND US

When we ask our mother how long we'll be
    here,
sometimes she says *for a while* and
    sometimes
she tells us not to ask anymore
because she doesn't know how long we'll
    stay
in the house where she grew up
on the land she's always known.

When we ask, she tells us
this is where she used to belong
but her sister, Caroline, our aunt Kay, has
    moved
to the North,
her brother Odell is dead now,
and her baby brother, Robert, says he's
    almost saved
enough money to follow Caroline to New
    York City.

Maybe I should go there, too, my mother
   says.
Everyone else, she says,
has a new place to be now.

Everyone else
has gone away.
And now coming back home
isn't really coming back home
at all.

THE GARDEN

Each spring
the dark Nicholtown dirt is filled
with the promise
of what the earth can give back to you
if you work the land
plant the seeds
pull the weeds.

My southern grandfather missed slavery
by one generation. His grandfather
had been owned.
His father worked
the land from dawn till dusk
for the promise of cotton
and a little pay.

So this is what he believes in
your hands in the cool dirt
until the earth gives back to you
all that you've asked of it.

Sweet peas and collards,
green peppers and cukes
lettuce and melon,

berries and peaches and one day
when I'm able, my grandfather says,
*I'm gonna figure out how to grow myself a
   pecan tree.*

God gives you what you need, my
   grandmother says.
Best not to ask for more than that.

Hmph, my grandfather says. And goes back
to working the land, pulling from it all we
   need

and more than that.

Gunnar's Children

At dusk, just as the fireflies flicker on, my
    grandfather
makes his way
home.
We see him coming slow down the road,
his silver lunch box bouncing
soft against his leg. Now,
as he gets closer, we hear him
singing:

"Where will the wedding supper be?
Way down yonder in a hollow tree. Uh
    hmmm . . ."

Good evening, Miz Clara. Evening, Miz Mae.
How's that leg, Miz Bell?
What you cooking, Auntie Charlotte, you
    thinking
of making me something to eat?
His voice ringing down Hall Street, circling
round the roads of Nicholtown
and maybe out into the big, wide

world . . .

Maybe all the way up in New York,
Aunt Kay's hearing it,
and thinking about coming on home . . .
Then he is close enough to run to — the
   three of us
climbing him like a tree until he laughs out
   loud.

We call him Daddy.
This is what our mother calls him.
This is all we know now.

Our daddy seems taller than anyone else
in all of Greenville.
More handsome, too —
His square jaw and light brown eyes
so different from our own
narrow-faced, dark-eyed selves. Still,
his hand is warm and strong around my
   own
   as I skip beside him,
the wind blowing up around us. He says,
Y'all are Gunnar's children.
Just keep remembering that.

Just keep remembering . . .

This is the way of Nicholtown evenings,

Daddy
coming home,

me
jumping into his arms,
the others
circling around him
all of us grinning
all of us talking
all of us loving him up.

AT THE END OF THE DAY

There are white men working at the
  printing press
beside Daddy, their fingers blackened
with ink so that at the end of the day,
  palms up
it's hard to tell who is white and who is
  not, still
they call my grandfather Gunnar,
even though he's a foreman
and is supposed to be called
Mr. Irby.
But he looks the white men in the eye
sees the way so many of them can't
  understand
a colored man
telling them what they need to do.
This is new. Too fast for them.
The South is changing.

Sometimes they don't listen.
Sometimes they walk away.

At the end of the day, the newspaper is
   printed,
the machines are shut down and each man
punches a clock and leaves but

only Colored folks
come home to Nicholtown.

Here, you can't look right or left or up or
   down
without seeing brown people.
Colored Town. Brown Town. Even a few
   mean words
to say where we live.

My grandmother tells us
it's the way of the South. *Colored folks used
   to stay*
where they were told that they belonged. But
times are changing.
And people are itching to go where they
   want.

This evening, though,
I am happy to belong
to Nicholtown.

DAYWORK

There is daywork for colored women.
In the mornings their dark bodies
fill the crosstown buses,
taking them away
from Nicholtown
to the other side
of Greenville
where the white people live.
Our grandmother tells us this
as she sets a small hat with a topaz pin on
  her head,
pulls white gloves
over her soft brown hands.
Two days a week, she joins the women,
taking on this second job now
that there are four more mouths to feed
and the money
she gets from part-time teaching isn't
  enough
anymore. *I'm not ashamed,* she says,
cleaning is what I know. I'm not ashamed,

if it feeds my children.

When she returns in the evening, her
  hands
are ashen from washing other people's
  clothes,
Most often by hand,
her ankles swollen from standing all day
making beds and sweeping floors,
shaking dust from curtains,
picking up after other people's children,
  cooking,
the list
goes on and on.
Don't any of you ever do daywork, she warns
  us.
I'm doing it now so you don't have to.
And maybe all across Nicholtown, other
  children
are hearing this, too.

Get the Epsom salts, she says, leaning back
into the soft brown chair, her eyes closing.
When she isn't in it, Hope, Dell and I
  squeeze in
side by side by side and still, there is space
  left
for one more.
We fill a dishpan with warm water, pour
the salts in, swirl it around and carefully

72

carry it to her feet. We fight to see who will
   get
to rub the swelling from my grandmother's
   ankles,
the smile back onto her face,
the stories back into the too-quiet room.

You could have eaten off the floor by the
   time
I left this one house today,
my grandmother begins, letting out a heavy
   sigh. *But*
let me tell you,
when I first got there, you would have
   thought
the Devil himself had come through . . .

LULLABY

At night, every living thing competes
for a chance to be heard.
The crickets
and frogs call out.
Sometimes, there's the soft
who-whoo of an owl lost
amid the pines.
Even the dogs won't rest until
they've howled
at the moon.

But the crickets always win, long after
the frogs stop croaking
and the owl has found its way home.
Long after the dogs have lain down
losing the battle against sleep,
the crickets keep going
as though they know their song
is our lullaby.

BIBLE TIMES

My grandmother keeps her Bible on a shelf
beside her bed. When the day is over,
she reads quietly to herself, and in the
  morning
she'll tell us the stories,
how Noah listened
to God's word
pulled two of each animal inside his ark,
  waited
for the rains to come and floated safely
as the sinners drowned.

It's morning now and we have floated
  safely
through the Nicholtown night,
our evening prayers
Jehovah, please give us another day,
now answered.
Biscuits warm and buttered stop halfway
to our mouths. *How much rain did it take*
to destroy the sinners? What lies did they tell

to die such a death? How loud was the rain
when it came? How did Noah know
that the cobra wouldn't bite, the bull
wouldn't charge, the bee wouldn't sting?

Our questions come fast but we want
the stories more than we want the answers
so when my grandmother says,
Hush, so I can tell it!
We do.
Jacob's dream of a ladder to heaven, and
    Jesus
with the children surrounding him. Moses
on the mountain, fire burning words into
    stone.
Even Salome intrigues us, her wish for a
    man's head
on a platter — who could want this and
    live
to tell the story of that wanting?

Autumn is coming.
Outside, there's the sound of wind
through the pine trees.
But inside there are stories, there are
    biscuits
and grits and eggs, the fire in the
    potbellied stove
already filling the house with warmth.

Still we shiver at the thought of evil
   Salome,
chew our biscuits slowly.
We are safe here — miles and years away
from Bible Times.

THE READER

When we can't find my sister, we know
she is under the kitchen table, a book in
  her hand,
a glass of milk and a small bowl of peanuts
  beside her.

We know we can call Odella's name out
  loud,
slap the table hard with our hands,
dance around it singing
"She'll Be Coming 'Round the Mountain"
so many times the song makes us sick
and the circling makes us dizzy
and still
my sister will do nothing more
than slowly turn the page.

THE BEGINNING

I cannot write a word yet but at three,
I now know the letter *J*
love the way it curves into a hook
that I carefully top with a straight hat
the way my sister has taught me to do.
  Love
the sound of the letter and the promise
that one day this will be connected to a full
  name,

my own

that I will be able to write

by myself.

Without my sister's hand over mine,
making it do what I cannot yet do.

How amazing these words are that slowly
  come to me.

How wonderfully on and on they go.

Will the words end, I ask
whenever I remember to.

Nope, my sister says, all of five years old
   now,
and promising me

infinity.

HOPE

The South doesn't agree
with my brother.
The heat sandpapers his skin.
Don't scratch, my grandmother warns. But
  he does
and the skin grows raw beneath his fingers.
The pollen leaves him puffy eyed, his small
  breaths
come quick, have too much sound around
  them.
He moves slow, sickly now where once
he was strong.
And when his body isn't betraying him,
  Ohio does.
The memories waking him in the night, the
  view
from my father's shoulders, the wonder
of the Nelsonville house, the air
so easy to breathe . . .

You can keep your South, my father had
  said.

Now Hope stays mostly quiet
unless asked to speak, his head bent
inside the superhero comic books my
  grandfather
brings home on Fridays. Hope searches for
  himself
inside their pages. Leaves them
dog-eared by Monday morning.

The South
his mortal enemy.
The South,
his Kryptonite.

THE ALMOST FRIENDS

There's the boy from up the road
with the hole in his heart. Some afternoons
he comes to sit in our yard and listen
to our stories. Our aunt Kay, we tell him,
lives in New York City and maybe we will,
   too,
someday. And yes it's true, once
we lived in Ohio, that's why
we speak the way we do.
We don't ask about the hole
in his heart. Our grandmother warns us
we know better than that.

There is Cora and her sisters, across the
   road.
One word in my grandmother's mouth —
   You stay away
from Coraandhersisters, their mother
left the family, ran off
with their church pastor.
Coraandhersisters

sometimes
sit watching us.
We watch them back not asking
what it feels like not to have a mother
   because
our grandmother warns us
we know better than that.

There are three brothers who live down
   the road
we know this only because
our grandmother tells us. They live
inside their dark house
all summer, coming out
in the evening when their mother returns
   from work
long after we've bathed and slipped into
our summer pajamas, books curled into
our arms.

These are our almost friends, the people
we think about when we're tired of
   playing
with each other.

But our grandmother says,
Three is plenty. Three is a team.
Find something to do together.
And so over and over again,
we do. Even though we want to ask her,

Why can't we play with them? we don't.

We know better than that.

THE RIGHT WAY TO SPEAK

The first time my brother says *ain't* my
  mother
pulls a branch from the willow tree
  growing down
the hill at the edge
of our backyard.
As she slips her closed hand over it,
removing the leaves,
my brother begins to cry
because the branch is a switch now

no longer beautifully weeping at the
  bottom of the hill.
It whirs as my mother whips it
through the air and down
against my brother's legs.

You will never, my mother says,
say ain't in this house.
You will never
say ain't anywhere.

Each switching is a warning to us
our words are to remain
crisp and clear.
We are never to say *huh?*
ain't or *y'all*
git or *gonna.*
Never *ma'am* — just *yes,* with eyes
meeting eyes enough
to show respect.
Don't ever ma'am anyone!
The word too painful
a memory for my mother
of not-so-long-ago
southern subservient days . . .

The list of what not to say
goes on and on . . .

You are from the North, our mother says.
You know the right way to speak.

As the switch raises dark welts on my
  brother's legs
Dell and I look on
afraid to open our mouths. Fearing the
  South
will slip out or
into them.

THE CANDY LADY

On Fridays, our grandfather takes us
to the candy lady's house,
even though our grandmother worries he's
   going
to be the cause of our teeth rotting
right out of our heads.
But my grandfather just laughs,
makes us open our mouths
to show the strong Irby teeth we've
   inherited
from *his* side of the family.
The three of us stand there, our mouths
   open wide,
strong white teeth inside,
and my grandmother has to nod, has to
   say,
They're lucky before sending us on our way.

The candy lady's small living room is filled
with shelves and shelves of chocolate bars
and gumdrops, Good & Plenty and Jujubes,

Moon Pies and Necco Wafers,
lollipops and long red licorice strings.
So much candy that it's hard to choose
until our grandfather says,
Get what you want but I'm getting myself
  some ice cream.

Then the candy lady, who is gray-haired
and never smiles, disappears
into another room and returns a few
  minutes later
with a wafer cone, pale yellow
lemon-chiffon ice cream dripping from it.
Outside, even this late in the afternoon,
the sun is beating down
and the idea of lemon-chiffon ice cream
  cooling us,
even for a few minutes,
makes us all start saying at once — *Me,*
  too, Daddy.
Me, too, Daddy. Me, too.

The walk home from the candy lady's
  house
is a quiet one
except for the sound of melting ice cream
being slurped up
fast, before it slides past our wrists,
on down our arms and onto
the hot, dry road.

SOUTH CAROLINA AT WAR

Because we have a right, my grandfather
  tells us —
we are sitting at his feet and the story
  tonight is

why people are marching all over the
  South —

to walk and sit and dream wherever we want.

First they brought us here.
Then we worked for free. Then it was 1863,
and we were supposed to be free but we
  weren't.

And that's why people are so mad.

And it's true, we can't turn on the radio
without hearing about the marching.

We can't go to downtown Greenville
  without

90

seeing the teenagers walking into stores, sitting
where brown people still aren't allowed to sit
and getting carried out, their bodies limp, their faces calm.

This is the way brown people have to fight,
my grandfather says.
You can't just put your fist up. You have to insist
on something
gently. Walk toward a thing
slowly.

But be ready to die,
my grandfather says,
for what is right.

Be ready to die, my grandfather says,
for everything you believe in.

And none of us can imagine death
but we try to imagine it anyway.

Even my mother joins the fight.
When she thinks our grandmother
isn't watching she sneaks out
to meet the cousins downtown, but just as
she's stepping through the door,

her good dress and gloves on, my
  grandmother says,
Now don't go getting arrested.
And Mama sounds like a little girl when
  she says,
I won't.

More than a hundred years, my grandfather
  says,
and we're still fighting for the free life
we're supposed to be living.

So there's a war going on in South
  Carolina
and even as we play
and plant and preach and sleep, we are a
  part of it.

Because you're colored, my grandfather
  says.
And just as good and bright and beautiful
  and free
as anybody.
And nobody colored in the South is stopping,
my grandfather says,
until everybody knows what's true.

THE TRAINING

When my mother's older cousin
and best friend, Dorothy,
comes with her children, they run off
saying they can't understand
the way Hope, Dell and I speak.
Y'all go too fast, they say.
And the words get all pushed together.
They say they don't feel like playing
with us little kids. So they leave us
to walk the streets of Nicholtown when we
    can't
leave the porch.
We watch them go, hear
Cousin Dorothy say, *Don't you
    knuckleheads
get into trouble out there.*
Then we stay close to Cousin Dorothy,
    make believe
we're not listening when she knows we are.
Laughing when she laughs, shaking our
    own heads

93

when she shakes
hers. *You know how you have to get those trainings,*
she says, and our mother nods. *They won't let you sit at the counters without them. Have to know what to do when those people come at you.*
She has a small space between her teeth
like my mother's space, and Hope's and Dell's, too.
She is tall and dark-skinned,
beautiful and broad shouldered.
She wears gloves and dark-colored dresses made for her
by a seamstress in Charleston.

The trainings take place in the basements of churches
and the back rooms of stores,
on long car trips and anywhere else where people can
gather. They learn
how to change the South without violence,
how to not be moved
by the evil actions of others, how to walk slowly but
with deliberate steps.
How to sit at counters and be cursed at
without cursing back, have food and drinks poured

over them without standing up and hurting
  someone.
Even the teenagers
get trained to sit tall, not cry, swallow back
  fear.

But Lord, Cousin Dorothy says. *Everybody*
  has a line.
When I'm walking
up to that lunch counter and taking my seat,
I pray to God, don't let
anybody spit on me. I can be Sweet Dorothy
seven days a week, twenty-four hours a day
as long as nobody crosses that line. Because
  if they do,
this nonviolent movement

is over!

THE BLANKET

The first time my mother goes to New York
   City
it is only for a long-weekend visit,
her kiss on our cheeks
as much a promise as the excitement in her
   eyes.
I'll bring something back for each of you.

It's Friday night and the weekend ahead
is already calling us
to the candy lady's house,
my hand in Daddy's.
He doesn't know how to say no,
my grandmother complains.

But neither does she,
dresses and socks and ribbons,
our hair pressed and curled.
She calls my sister and me her baby girls,
smiles proudly when the women say how
   pretty we are.

So the first time my mother goes to New
  York City
we don't know to be sad, the weight
of our grandparents' love like a blanket
with us beneath it,
safe and warm.

Miss Bell and
the Marchers

They look like regular people
visiting our neighbor Miss Bell,
foil-covered dishes held out in front of
   them
as they arrive
some in pairs,
some alone,
some just little kids
holding their mothers' hands.

If you didn't know, you'd think it was just
an evening gathering. Maybe church people
heading into Miss Bell's house to talk
about God. But when Miss Bell pulls her
   blinds
closed, the people fill their dinner plates
   with food,
their glasses with sweet tea and gather
to talk about marching.

And even though Miss Bell works for a

white lady
who said *I will fire you in a minute if I ever
  see you
on that line!*
Miss Bell knows that marching isn't the
  only thing
she can do,
knows that people fighting need full bellies
  to think
and safe places to gather.
She knows the white lady isn't the only one
who's watching, listening, waiting,
to end this fight. So she keeps the
  marchers'
glasses filled, adds more corn bread
and potato salad to their plates,
stands in the kitchen ready to slice
lemon pound cake into generous pieces.

And in the morning, just before she pulls
her uniform from the closet, she prays,
*God, please give me and those people
  marching
another day.*

Amen.

How to Listen #2

In the stores downtown
we're always followed around
just because we're brown.

HAIR NIGHT

Saturday night smells of biscuits and
  burning hair.
Supper done and my grandmother has
  transformed
the kitchen into a beauty shop. Laid across
  the table
is the hot comb, Dixie Peach hair grease,
horsehair brush, parting stick
and one girl at a time.
Jackie first, my sister says,
our freshly washed hair damp
and spiraling over toweled shoulders
and pale cotton nightgowns.
She opens her book to the marked page,
curls up in a chair pulled close
to the wood-burning stove, bowl of peanuts
  in her lap.
The words
in her books are so small, I have to squint
to see the letters. *Hans Brinker or The Silver
  Skates.*

*The House at Pooh Corner. Swiss Family
    Robinson.*
Thick books
dog-eared from the handing down from
    neighbor
to neighbor. My sister handles them gently,
marks the pages with torn brown pieces
of paper bag, wipes her hands before going
beyond the hardbound covers.
Read to me, I say, my eyes and scalp
    already stinging
from the tug of the brush through my hair.
And while my grandmother sets the hot
    comb
on the flame, heats it just enough to pull
my tight curls straighter, my sister's voice
wafts over the kitchen,
past the smell of hair and oil and flame,
    settles
like a hand on my shoulder and holds me
    there.
I want silver skates like Hans's, a place
on a desert island. I have never seen the
    ocean
but this, too, I can imagine — blue water
    pouring
over red dirt.
As my sister reads, the pictures begin
    forming
as though someone has turned on a

television,
lowered the sound,
pulled it up close.
Grainy black-and-white pictures come
   slowly at me
Deep. Infinite. Remembered

On a bright December morning long ago . . .

My sister's clear soft voice opens up the
   world to me.
I lean in
so hungry for it.

Hold still now, my grandmother warns.
So I sit on my hands to keep my mind
off my hurting head, and my whole body
   still.
But the rest of me is already leaving,
the rest of me is already gone.

FAMILY NAMES

There's James, Joseph, Andrew, Geneva,
 Annie Mae,
William, Lucinda, David, Talmudge,
my grandmother says. *All together,*
my mama gave birth to thirteen children.
Our heads spin at the thought of that many
 brothers
and sisters. *Three died as babies,* she says,
but only a little of the spinning stops.

There's Levonia, Montague, Iellus,
 Hallique,
Valie Mae, Virdie and Elora on my daddy's
 side.
We can't help but laugh each time our
 daddy
tells us the names of his brothers and
 sisters.
His own name,
Gunnar, sends us laughing all over again.
Gave their kids names

that no master could ever take away.
What about Bob or Joe? Hope wants to
  know.
What about
John or Michael? Or something real normal,
  like Hope?
Hope is not normal, my sister says. *Not for a*
  boy. I think
your name is a mistake. Maybe they meant
to name you Virdie.

I'm the great Hope of the family, my brother
  says.
Just like Grandpa Hope.
Just like Hope the Dope, my sister says
  back.

Keep up the arguing, my grandfather says,
I'll take you both down to city hall.
People be happy to call you Talmudge and
  Valie Mae.

American Dream

Even when my girls were little, we'd go down
  there,
my grandmother tells us. *And people'd be*
  marching.
The marching didn't just start yesterday.
Police with those dogs, scared everybody
near to death. Just once
I let my girls march.

My grandmother leans back in her brown
  chair,
her feet still in the Epsom salts water,
her fingers tapping out
some silent tune. She closes her eyes.
I let them and I prayed.

What's the thing, I ask her, *that would make*
  people
want to live together?

People have to want it, that's all.

We get quiet — maybe all of us are
   thinking about
the ones who want it. And the ones who
   don't.

We all have the same dream, my
   grandmother says.
*To live equal in a country that's supposed to
   be*
the land of the free.
She lets out a long breath,
deep remembering.

When your mother was little
she wanted a dog. But I said no.
Quick as you can blink, I told her,
a dog will turn on you.

So my mother brought kittens home,
soft and purring inside of empty boxes
mewing and mewing until my grandmother
fell in love. And let her keep them.

My grandmother tells us all this
as we sit at her feet, each story like a
   photograph
we can look right into, see our mother
   there
marchers and dogs and kittens all blending
and us now

there in each moment
beside her.

THE FABRIC STORE

Some Fridays, we walk to downtown
  Greenville where
there are some clothing stores, some
  restaurants,
a motel and the five-and-dime store but
my grandmother won't take us
into any of those places anymore.
Even the five-and-dime, which isn't
  segregated now
but where a woman is paid, my
  grandmother says,
to follow colored people around in case
  they try to
steal something. We don't go into the
  restaurants
because they always seat us near the
  kitchen.
When we go downtown,
we go to the fabric store, where the white
  woman
knows my grandmother

from back in Anderson, asks,
*How's Gunnar doing and your girls in New
York?*
She rolls fabric out for my grandmother
to rub between her fingers.
They discuss drape and nap and where to
cinch
the waist on a skirt for a child.
At the fabric store, we are not Colored
or Negro. We are not thieves or shameful
or something to be hidden away.
At the fabric store, we're just people.

GHOSTS

In downtown Greenville,
they painted over the WHITE ONLY signs,
except on the bathroom doors,
they didn't use a lot of paint
so you can still see the words, right there
like a ghost standing in front
still keeping you out.

THE LEAVERS

We watch men leave Greenville
in their one good suit, shoes
spit shined.
We watch women leave in Sunday clothes,
hatted and lipsticked and white gloved.

We watch them catch buses in the evening,
the black shadows of their backs
the last we see of them.
Others fill their cars with bags.
Whole families disappearing into the night.
People waving good-bye.

They say the City is a place where
  diamonds
speckle the sidewalk. Money
falls from the sky.
They say a colored person can do well
  going there.
All you need is the fare out of Greenville.
All you need is to know somebody on the

other side,
waiting to cross you over.

Like the River Jordan

and then you're in Paradise.

THE BEGINNING
OF THE LEAVING

When my mother returns from New York
she has a new plan — all of us are going
to move there. We don't know
anyplace else but Greenville now — New
  York
is only the pictures she shows us
in magazines and the two she has in her
  pocketbook
of our aunt Kay. In one, there are two
  other people
standing with her.
Bernie and Peaches, our mother tells us.
  We all used to be friends
here in Nicholtown.
That's all the young kids used to talk about,
our grandmother tells us,
going to New York City.

My mother smiles at us and says,
We'll be going to New York City.
I just have to figure some things out first,

that's all.

I don't know what I'd do without you all up
  under me,
my grandmother says and there's a sadness
in her voice.
Don't know what I'd do, she says again.
Even sadder this time.

As a Child,
I Smelled the Air

Mama takes her coffee out to the front
  porch
sips it slow. Two steps down and her feet
are covered in grass and dew.
New York doesn't smell like this, she says.

I follow her, the dew cool against my feet
the soft hush of wind through leaves
my mother and I
alone together.

Her coffee is sweetened with condensed
  milk,
her hair pulled back into a braid,
her dark fingers circling her cup.
If I ask, she will hold it to my lips,
let me taste the bittersweet of it.

It's dawn and the birds have come alive,
  chasing
each other from maple to pine and back

to maple again. This is how time passes
  here.
The maple will be bare-branched come
  winter,
Mama says. *But the pines, they just keep on*
  living.

And the air is what I'll remember.
Even once we move to New York.
It always smelled like this, my mother says.
Wet grass and pine.

Like memory.

Harvest Time

When Daddy's garden is ready
it is filled with words that make me laugh
when I say them —
pole beans and *tomatoes, okra* and *corn*
sweet peas and *sugar snaps,*
lettuce and *squash.*

Who could have imagined

so much color that the ground disappears
and we are left
walking through an autumn's worth
of crazy words
that beneath the magic
of my grandmother's hands

become

side dishes.

Grown Folks' Stories

Warm autumn night with the crickets
   crying
the smell of pine coming soft on the wind
and the women
on the porch, quilts across their laps,
Aunt Lucinda, Miss Bell and whatever
   neighbor
has a *breath or two left* at the end of the
   day
for *sitting and running our mouths.*

That's when we listen
to the grown folks talking.
Hope, Dell and me sitting quiet on the
   stairs.
We know one word from us will bring a
   hush
upon the women, my grandmother's finger
   suddenly
pointing toward the house, her soft-spoken
I think it's time for you kids to go to bed now

ushering
us into our room. So we are silent, our
     backs against
posts and the back of the stairs, Hope's
     elbows
on his knees, head down. Now is when we
     learn
everything
there is to know
about the people down the road and
in the daywork houses,
about the Sisters at the Kingdom Hall
and the faraway relatives we rarely see.

Long after the stories are told, I remember
     them,
whisper them back to Hope
and Dell late into the night:
She's the one who left Nicholtown in the
     daytime
the one Grandmama says wasn't afraid
of anything. Retelling each story.
Making up what I didn't understand
or missed when voices dropped too low, I
     talk
until my sister and brother's soft breaths
     tell me
they've fallen
asleep.

Then I let the stories live
inside my head, again and again
until the real world fades back
into cricket lullabies
and my own dreams.

TOBACCO

Summer is over, a kiss
of chill in the southern air. We see the dim
  orange
of my grandfather's cigarette, as he makes
  his way
down the darkening road. Hear his evening
  greetings
and the coughing that follows them.
Not enough breath left now
to sing so I sing for him, in my head
where only I can hear.

Where will the wedding supper be?
Way down yonder in a hollow tree. Uh
  hmmm . . .

The old people used to say
a pinch of dirt in the mouth
can tell tobacco's story:
what crops
are ready for picking

what needs to be left to grow.
What soil is rich enough for planting
and the patches of land that need
a year of rest.

I do not know yet
how sometimes the earth makes a promise
it can never keep. Tobacco fields
lay fallow, crops picked clean.
My grandfather coughs again
and the earth waits

for what and who it will get in return.

How to Listen #3

Middle of the night
my grandfather is coughing
me upright. Startled.

My Mother
Leaving Greenville

It is late autumn now, the smell of wood
  burning,
the potbellied stove like a warm soft hand
in the center of my grandparents' living
  room,
its black pipe
stretching into the ceiling then
  disappearing.

So many years have passed since we last
  saw
our father, his absence
like a bubble in my older brother's life,
that pops again and again
into a whole lot of tiny bubbles
of memory.

You were just a baby, he says to me.
*You're so lucky you don't remember the
  fighting
or anything.*

It's like erasers came through her memory,
  my sister says.
Erase. Erase. Erase.

But now, my mother is leaving again.

This, I will remember.

Halfway Home #1

New York, my mother says.
Soon, I'll find us a place there. Come back
and bring you all home.

She wants a place of her own that is not
The Nelsonville House, The Columbus
  House,
The Greenville House.
Looking for her next place.
Our next place.
Right now, our mother says,
we're only halfway home.

And I imagine her standing
in the middle of a road, her arms out
fingers pointing North and South.

I want to ask:
Will there always be a road?
Will there always be a bus?
Will we always have to choose

between home

and home?

MY MOTHER LOOKS BACK
ON GREENVILLE

After our dinner and bath,
after our powdered and pajamaed bodies
   are tucked
three across into bed,
after *Winnie the Pooh* and kisses on our
   foreheads
and longer-than-usual hugs,

my mother walks away from the house on
   Hall Street
out into the growing night,
down a long dusty road
to where the Nicholtown bus takes
her to the Greyhound station

then more dust

then she's gone.

New York ahead of her,
her family behind, she moves

to the back, her purse in her lap,
the land
pulling her gaze to the window once more.
Before darkness
covers it and for many hours, there are
  only shadows

and stars

and tears

and hope.

THE LAST FIREFLIES

We know our days are counted here.
Each evening we wait for the first light
of the last fireflies, catch them in jars
then let them go again. As though we
  understand
their need for freedom.
As though our silent prayers to stay in
  Greenville
will be answered if
we do what we know is right.

CHANGES

Now the evenings are quiet with my
   mother gone
as though the night is listening
to the way we are counting the days. We
   know
even the feel of our grandmother's brush
being pulled gently through our hair
will fast become a memory. Those Saturday
   evenings
at her kitchen table, the smell
of Dixie Peach hair grease,
the sizzle of the straightening comb,
the hiss of the iron
against damp, newly washed ribbons, all of
   this
may happen again, but in another place.

We sit on our grandparents' porch,
shivering already against the coming
   winter,
and talk softly about Greenville summer,

how when we come back,
we'll do all the stuff we always did,
hear the same stories,
laugh at the same jokes, catch fireflies in
  the same
mason jars, promise each other
future summers that are as good as the
  past.
But we know we are lying

coming home will be different now.

This place called Greenville
this neighborhood called Nicholtown
will change some

and so will each of us.

STERLING HIGH SCHOOL, GREENVILLE

While my mother is away in New York
    City,
a fire sweeps through
her old high school
during a senior dance.

Smoke filled the crowded room
and the music
stopped
and the students dancing
stopped
and the DJ told them
to quickly leave the building.

The fire
lasted all night
and when it was over,
my mother's high school had burned
nearly to the ground.

My mother said it was because

the students had been marching,
and the marching
made some white people in Greenville
  mad.

After the fire the students weren't allowed
  to go to
the all-white high school.
Instead they had to crowd in
beside their younger sisters and brothers
at the lower school.

In the photos from my mother's high
  school yearbook —
               The Torch, 1959,
my mother is smiling beside her cousin
Dorothy Ann and on her other side,
there is Jesse Jackson,
who maybe was already dreaming of one
  day
being the first brown man to run
for president.

And not even
the torching of their school
could stop him or the marchers
from changing the world.

FAITH

After my mother leaves, my grandmother
pulls us further
into the religion she has always known.
We become Jehovah's Witnesses
like her.

After my mother leaves
there is no one
to say,
*The children can choose their own faith
when they're old enough.
In my house,* my grandmother says,
you will do as I do.

After my mother leaves,
we wake in the middle of the night
calling out for her.
Have faith, my grandmother
says pulling us to her in the darkness.

Let the Bible,

my grandmother says,
become your sword and your shield.
But we do not know yet
who we are fighting
and what we are fighting for.

THE STORIES CORA TELLS

In the evening now
Coraandhersisters come over to our porch.
There are three of them
and three of us but Hope
moves away from the girls
sits by himself
out in the yard.

And even though my grandmother tells us
not to play with them,
she doesn't call us into the house anymore
when she sees them walking down the
  road. Maybe
her heart moves over a bit
making room for them.

A colorful mushroom grows
beneath the pine tree. Purple and gold and
  strange
against the pine-needled ground.
When I step on it,

Coraandhersisters scream at me,
You just killed the Devil while he was
  sleeping!
Sleeping in his own house.

Cora warns me
the Devil will soon be alive again.
She says, *He's going to come for you,*
late in the night while you're sleeping
and the God y'all pray to won't be there
  protecting you.

I cry as the sun sets, waiting.
Cry until my grandmother comes out
shoos Coraandhersisters home
holds me tight
tells me they are lying.
That's just some crazy southern superstition,
my grandmother says.
Those girls must be a little simple not
  knowing
a mushroom when they see one.
Don't believe everything you hear, Jackie.
Someday, you'll come to know
when someone is telling the truth
and when they're just making up stories.

HALL STREET

In the early evening, just before the best
  light
for hide-and-seek
takes over the sky,
it's Bible-study time. We watch
from our places on the front porch, our
  cold hands
cupped around hot chocolate
half gone and sweetest at the bottom
as the Brother and Sister
from the Kingdom Hall make their way up
  our road.

Pretty Monday evening, the Brother
from the Kingdom Hall says.
Thank Jehovah, the Sister
from the Kingdom Hall says back.
We are silent, Brother Hope, Sister Dell
  and me.

None of us want to sit inside when the late

autumn
is calling to us
and frogs are finally feeling brave enough
to hop across our yard. We want
anything but this. We want warm biscuits
and tag and jacks on the porch,
our too-long sweater sleeves
getting in the way sometimes.

But we are Jehovah's Witnesses. Monday
    night
is Bible-study time.

Somewhere else,
my grandfather is
spending time with his brother Vertie.
Maybe they are playing the harmonica and
    banjo,
laughing and singing loud. Doing
what's fun to do on a pretty Monday
    evening.

*Jehovah promises us everlasting life in the
    New World,*
the Brother from the Kingdom Hall says
and Brother Hope, Sister Dell and me are
    silent
wanting only what's right outside.
Wanting only this world.

SOON

When the phone rings in my
  grandmother's kitchen,
we run from wherever we are,
jumping from the front porch swing
climbing out of the mud-filled ditch out
  back,
running quick from the picked-clean
  garden —
but
my brother, Hope, is the fastest, picking up
  the phone,
pressing it hard
against his ear as though my mother's voice
just that much closer means my mother is
closer to us. We jump around him:
Let me speak! until my grandmother comes
through the screen door
puts down the basket of laundry, cold and
  dry
from the line
takes the phone from my brother,

shushes us,
shoos us,
promises us

a moment with our mother soon.

How I Learn
the Days of the Week

Monday night is Bible study with a Brother
and Sister
from the Kingdom Hall.

Tuesday night is Bible study at the
Kingdom Hall.

Wednesday night is laundry night — the
clothes
blowing clean on the line above
my grandfather's garden. When no one is
looking,
we run through the sheets,
breathe in all the wonderful smells the air
adds to them.

Thursday night is Ministry School. One
day,
we will grow up to preach
God's word, take it out
into the world

and maybe we'll save some people.

Friday night, we're free as anything,
Hope and Dell's bikes skidding along Hall
    Street,
my knees bumping hard against the
    handlebars
of my red three-wheeler. One more year
    maybe
Dell's bike will be mine.

Saturday we're up early: *The Watchtower*
    and *Awake!*
in our hands, we walk like sleepy soldiers
through Nicholtown, ringing bells,
    knocking on doors,
spreading the good news
of something better coming. Sometimes,
the people listen.
Sometimes, they slam their doors
or don't open them at all. Or look sadly
    down at me
ribboned and starched, my face clean and
    shining
with oil, my words earnest as anything:
*Good morning, I'm Sister Jacqueline and I'm
    here*
to bring you some good news today.
Sometimes they give me a dime but won't
    take

my *Watchtower* and *Awake!*

Sunday it's *Watchtower* study at the
  Kingdom Hall,
two hours
of sitting and sitting and sitting.

Then Monday comes and the week starts
all over again.

RIBBONS

They are pale blue or pink or white.
They are neatly ironed each Saturday
  night.
Come Sunday morning, they are tied to
  the braids
hanging down past our ears.

We wear ribbons every day except Saturday
when we wash them by hand, Dell and I
side by side at the kitchen sink,
rubbing them with Ivory soap then rinsing
  them
beneath cool water.
Each of us
dreaming of the day our grandmother says
You're too old for ribbons.

But it feels like that day will never come.

When we hang them on the line to dry, we
  hope

they'll blow away in the night breeze
but they don't. Come morning, they're
   right
where we left them
gently moving in the cool air, eager to
   anchor us
to childhood.

Two Gods.
Two Worlds

It's barely morning and we're already
  awake,
my grandmother in the kitchen ironing
our Sunday clothes.

I can hear Daddy coughing in his bed, a
  cough like
he'll never catch his breath. The sound
  catches
in my chest as I'm pulling my dress
over my head. Hold my own breath
until the coughing stops. Still,
I hear him pad through the living room
hear the squeak of the front screen door
  and
know, he's made it to the porch swing,
to smoke a cigarette.

My grandfather doesn't believe in a God
that won't let him smoke
or have a cold beer on a Friday night

a God that tells us all
the world is ending so that *Y'all walk*
  through this world
afraid as cats.
Your God is not my God, he says.

His cough moves through the air
back into our room where the light
is almost blue, the white winter sun
  painting it.
I wish the coughing would stop. I wish
he would put on Sunday clothes,
take my hand, walk with us
down the road.

Jehovah's Witnesses believe
that everyone who doesn't follow
God's word will be destroyed in a great
  battle called
Armageddon. And when the battle is done
there will be a fresh new world
a nicer more peaceful world.

But I want the world where my daddy is
and don't know why
anybody's God would make me
have to choose.

WHAT GOD KNOWS

We pray for my grandfather
ask God to spare him even though
he's a nonbeliever. We ask that Jehovah
   look
into his heart, see
the goodness there.

But my grandfather says he doesn't need
   our prayers.
I work hard, he says. *I treat people like I want
to be treated.
God sees this. God knows.*

At the end of the day
he lights a cigarette, unlaces
his dusty brogans. Stretches his legs.
God sees my good, he says.
*Do all the preaching and praying you want
but no need to do it for me.*

NEW PLAYMATES

Beautiful brown dolls come from New York
  City,
fancy stores my mother has walked
into. She writes of elevators, train stations,
buildings so high, they hurt
the neck to see.

She writes of places with beautiful names
Coney Island, Harlem, Brownsville, Bear
  Mountain.
She tells us she's seen the ocean, how the
  water
keeps going long after the eyes can't see it
  anymore
promises a whole other country
on the other side.

She tells us the toy stores are filled with
  dolls
  of every size and color
there's a barbershop and a hair salon

everywhere
you look
and a friend of Aunt Kay's saw Lena
    Horne
just walking down the street.

But only the dolls are real to us.

Their black hair in stiff curls down
over their shoulders,
their pink dresses made of crinoline and
    satin.
Their dark arms unbending.
Still
we hug their hard plastic close and imagine
they're calling us Mama
imagine they need us near.
Imagine the letters from our own
    mother —
Coming to get you soon —
are ones we're writing to them.
We will never leave you, we whisper.
They stare back at us,
blank-eyed and beautiful
silent and still.

DOWN THE ROAD

Be careful when you play with him,
my grandmother warns us about the boy
with the hole in his heart.
Don't make him run too fast. Or cry.

When he taps on our back door, we come
    out
sit quietly with him on the back stairs.
He doesn't talk much, this boy with the
    hole
in his heart
but when he does, it's to ask us about our
    mother
in New York City.

Is she afraid there?
Did she ever meet a movie star?
Do the buildings really
go on and on?

One day, he says — so soft, my brother,

154

sister and I
lean in to hear — *I'm gonna go to New York
City.*
Then he looks off, toward Cora's house
down the road.

That's south, my sister says. *New York's the
other way.*

GOD'S PROMISE

It is nearly Christmastime.
On the radio, a man with a soft deep voice
  is singing
telling us to have ourselves a merry
  little . . .

Nicholtown windows are filled with
  Christmas trees.
Coraandhersisters brag about what they are
  getting,
dolls and skates and swing sets. In the
  backyard
our own swing set is silent —
a thin layer of snow covering it.
When we are made to stay inside on
  Sunday
afternoons,
Coraandhersisters descend upon it, take
  the swings
up high,
stick their tongues out at us

as we stare from behind our glassed-in
  screen door.

Let them play, for heaven's sake, my
  grandmother says,
when we complain about them tearing it
  apart.
Your hearts are bigger than that!

But our hearts aren't bigger than that.
Our hearts are tiny and mad.
If our hearts were hands, they'd hit.
If our hearts were feet, they'd surely kick
  somebody!

THE OTHER INFINITY

We are the chosen people, our
   grandmother tells us.
*Everything we do is a part
of God's plan. Every breath you breathe is
   the gift God
is giving you. Everything we own . . .*

Daddy gave us the swings, my sister tells
   her. *Not God.*

My grandmother's words come slowly
   meaning
this lesson is an important one.

*With the money he earned by working at a
   job God
gave him a body strong enough to work with.*

Outside, our swing set is empty finally,
Coraandhersisters now gone.

Hope, Dell and I are silent.

158

So much we don't yet understand.
So much we don't yet believe.

But we know this:
Monday, Tuesday, Thursday,
Saturday and Sunday are reserved
for God's work. We are put here to do it
and we are expected to do it well.
What is promised to us in return

is eternity.

It's the same, my sister says,
or maybe even better than
infinity.

The empty swing set reminds us of this —
that what is bad won't be bad forever,
and what is good can sometimes last
a long, long time.

Even Coraandhersisters can only bother us
for a little while before they get called
    home
to supper.

SOMETIMES, NO WORDS ARE NEEDED

Deep winter and the night air is cold. So
  still,
it feels like the world goes on forever in the
  darkness
until you look up and the earth stops
in a ceiling of stars. My head against
my grandfather's arm,
a blanket around us as we sit on the front
  porch swing.
Its whine like a song.

You don't need words
on a night like this. Just the warmth
of your grandfather's arm. Just the silent
  promise
that the world as we know it
will always be here.

THE LETTER

The letter comes on a Saturday morning,
my sister opens it. My mother's
  handwriting
is easy, my sister says. *She doesn't write in
  script.*
She writes so we can understand her.

And then she reads my mother's letter
  slowly
while Hope and I sit at the kitchen table,
cheese grits near gone, scrambled eggs
leaving yellow dots
in our bowls. My grandmother's beloved
  biscuits
forgotten.
She's coming for us, my sister says and
  reads the part
where my mother tells her the plan.
We're really leaving Greenville, my sister
  says
and Hope sits up straighter

and smiles. But then the smile is gone.
How can we have both places?
How can we leave
all that we've known —
me on Daddy's lap in the early evening,
listening to Hope and Dell tell stories
about their lives at the small school
a mile down the road.
I will be five one day and the Nicholtown
    school
is a mystery
I'm just about to solve.

And what about the fireflies and ditches?
And what about the nights when
we all climb into our grandparents' bed
and they move apart, making room for us
in the middle.

And maybe that's when my sister reads the
    part
I don't hear:
a baby coming. Another one. A brother or
    sister.
Still in her belly but coming soon.

She's coming to get us, my sister says
    again,
looking around

162

our big yellow kitchen. Then running her
  hand
over the hardwood table
as though she's already gone
and trying to remember this.

ONE MORNING, LATE WINTER

Then one morning my grandfather is too
  sick
to walk the half mile to the bus
that takes him to work.

He stays in bed for the whole day
waking only to cough
and cough
and cough.

I walk slow around him
fluffing his pillows,
pressing cool cloths over his forehead
telling him the stories that come to me
again and again.

This I can do — find him another place to
  be
when this world is choking him.

Tell me a story, he says.

And I do.

New York Baby

When my mother returns,
I will no longer be her baby girl.
I am sitting on my grandmother's lap
when she tells me this,
already so tall my legs dangle far down, the
  tips
of my toes touching the porch mat. My
  head
rests on her shoulder now where once,
it came only to her collarbone. She smells
  the way
she always does, of Pine-Sol and cotton,
Dixie Peach hair grease and something
warm and powdery.

I want to know whose baby girl I'll be
when my mother's new baby comes, born
  where
the sidewalks sparkle and me just a regular
  girl.

I didn't know how much I loved
being everyone's baby girl
until now when my life as baby girl
is nearly over.

LEAVING GREENVILLE

My mother arrives in the middle of the
   night, and
sleepily, we pile into her arms and hold
   tight.

Her kiss on the top of my head reminds
   me
of all that I love.

Mostly her.

It is late winter but my grandmother keeps
the window in our room slightly open
so that the cold fresh air can move over us
as we sleep. Two thick quilts and the three
   of us
side by side by side.

This is all we know now —

Cold pine breezes, my grandmother's
    quilts,
the heat of the wood-burning stove, the
    sweet
slow voices of the people around us,
red dust wafting, then settling as though
    it's said
all that it needs to say.

My mother tucks us back into our bed
    whispering,
We have a home up North now.

I am too sleepy to tell her that Greenville is
    home.
That even in the wintertime, the crickets
sing us to sleep.

And tomorrow morning, you'll get to meet
your new baby brother.

But I am already mostly asleep again, two
    arms
wrapped tight
around my mama's hand.

ROMAN

His name is as strange as he is, this new
  baby brother
so pale and quiet and wide-eyed. He sucks
  his fist,
taking in all of us without blinking.
Another boy, Hope says,
now it's even-steven around here.

But I don't like the new baby of the family.
I want to send it back to wherever
babies live before they get here. When I
  pinch him,
a red mark stays behind, and his cry is high
  and tinny
a sound that hurts my ears.
That's what you get, my sister says.
His crying is him fighting you back.
Then she picks him up, holds him close,
tells him softly everything's all right,
everything's always going to be all right
until Roman gets quiet,

his wide black eyes looking only at Dell
as if
he believes her.

followed
the
sky's
mirrored
constellation
to
freedom

NEW YORK CITY

Maybe it's another New York City
the southerners talk about. Maybe that's
  where
there is money falling from the sky,
diamonds speckling
the sidewalks.

Here there is only gray rock, cold
and treeless as a bad dream. Who could
  love
this place — where no pine trees grow,
no porch swing moves
with the weight of
your grandmother.

This place is a Greyhound bus
humming through the night then letting
  out
a deep breath inside a place
called Port Authority. This place is a driver
  yelling,

New York City, last stop.
Everybody off.

This place is loud and strange
and nowhere I'm ever going to call
home.

BROOKLYN, NEW YORK

We did not stay in the small apartment
my mother found on Bristol Street,
Brownsville, Brooklyn, USA.

We did not stay because the dim bulb that
   hung
from a chain swung back and forth
when our upstairs neighbors walked
across their floor, casting shadows
that made my brother cry
and suck hard on his middle fingers.

We did not stay because the building was
   big and old
and when the bathroom ceiling fell
into the bathtub, my mother said,
*I am not Henny Penny and that is not the
   sky!*

So she called Aunt Kay and her boyfriend,
   Bernie,

they borrowed a truck and helped us pack,
bundled us up in winter coats
turned off that swinging light

and got us out of there!

HERZL STREET

So we moved to Herzl Street
where Aunt Kay and Bernie lived upstairs.
And Peaches from Greenville lived below
    us.

And on Saturday nights more people
from Greenville came by
sitting and running their mouths
while the pots on the stove bubbled
with collards and sizzled with chicken
and corn bread baked up brown
inside Kay's big black oven.

And the people from Greenville
brought people from Spartanburg
and Charleston
and all of them talked
like our grandparents talked
and ate what we ate

so they were red dirt and pine trees

they were fireflies in jelly jars
and lemon-chiffon ice cream cones.

They were laughter on hot city nights
hot milk on cold city mornings,
good food and good times
fancy dancing and soul music.

They were family.

THE JOHNNY PUMP

Some days we miss
the way the red dirt lifted up and landed
against our bare feet. Here
the sidewalks burn hot all summer long.
Here we wear shoes. Broken bottles
don't always get swept up right away.

But our block has three johnny pumps
and a guy with a wrench
to turn them on. On the days when the
    heat
stops your breath, he comes up the block
pulling it out of his pocket. Then the
    johnny pump
is blasting cool water everywhere
and us and other kids running through it,
refreshed and laughing.

Even the grown-ups come out sometimes.
Once, I saw my

never-ever-barefoot-outside-in-the-city
  mother
take off her sandals,
stand at the curb
and let the cool water run over her feet.
She was looking up at the tiny piece of sky.
And she was smiling.

GENETICS

My mother has a gap between
her two front teeth. So does Daddy
  Gunnar.
Each child in this family has the same
  space
connecting us.

Our baby brother, Roman, was born pale
  as dust.
His soft brown curls and eyelashes stop
people on the street.
Whose angel child is this? they want to
  know.
When I say, *My brother,* the people
wear doubt
thick as a cape
until we smile
and the cape falls.

Caroline but
We Called Her Aunt Kay,
Some Memories

Aunt Kay at the top of the stairs, her arms
    open,
her smile wide
and us running to her.

Aunt Kay dressed up on a Friday night
smelling of perfume,
her boyfriend, Bernie, her friend Peaches.

Aunt Kay in the kitchen with Peaches and
    Bernie
passing a blue-and-white box of Argo
    starch
back and forth, the hard white chunks of
    it,
disappearing into their mouths like candy,
the slow chew and swallow.

Aunt Kay and Mama and Peaches, in tight
    skirts
singing in a band.

Aunt Kay braiding my hair.

Aunt Kay running up the stairs to her own
  apartment
and me running behind her.

Aunt Kay laughing.

Aunt Kay hugging me.

Then a fall.
A crowd.
An ambulance.
My mother's tears.
A funeral.

And here, my Aunt Kay memories end.

MOVING AGAIN

After the falling
the stairs were all wrong to us.
Some days I head up there, my mother
  said,
forgetting that Kay is gone.

After the falling
Bernie and Peaches
packed their bags, moved out
to Far Rockaway, telling my mother
how much Kay loved the ocean.

After the falling
we took the A train
to their new apartment, played on the
  beach
till the sun went down, Mama quiet on a
  blanket
looking out at the water.

Kay was her big sister, only ten months
 older.
Everyone always thought they were twins
so that's what they said they were.
Couldn't look at one of us, my mother said,
without seeing the other.

After the falling
the hallway smelled
like Kay's perfume
whenever it rained

so we moved again
to the second floor of a pink house
on Madison Street.
Out front there was a five-foot sculpture
made from gray rock,
ivory and sand. A small fountain sent water
cascading over statues
of Mary, Joseph and Jesus.
People stopped in front of the house,
crossed themselves, mouthed a silent prayer
then moved on.

This house is protected, the landlord told
 my mother.
The saints keep us safe.
This house is protected, my mother
 whispered to us.
By the Saint of Ugly Sculpture.

187

After the falling
sometimes I would see my mother
smiling at that sculpture. And in her smile,
there was Aunt Kay's smile, the two of
    them
having a secret sister laugh, the two of
    them
together again.

COMPOSITION NOTEBOOK

And somehow, one day, it's just there
speckled black-and-white, the paper
inside smelling like something I could fall
  right into,
live there — inside those clean white pages.

I don't know how my first composition
  notebook
ended up in my hands, long before I could
  really write
someone must have known that this
was all I needed.

Hard not to smile as I held it, felt the
  breeze
as I fanned the pages.
My sister thought my standing there
smiling was crazy
didn't understand how the smell and feel
  and sight
of bright white paper

could bring me so much joy.

And why does she need a notebook? She
  can't even write!

For days and days, I could only sniff the
  pages,
hold the notebook close
listen to the sound the papers made.

Nothing in the world is like this —
a bright white page with
pale blue lines. The smell of a newly
  sharpened pencil
the soft hush of it
moving finally
one day
into letters.

And even though she's smarter than
  anything,
this is something
my sister can't even begin
to understand.

ON PAPER

The first time I write my full name

Jacqueline Amanda Woodson

without anybody's help
on a clean white page in my composition
    notebook,
    I know

if I wanted to

I could write anything.

Letters becoming words, words gathering
    meaning,
    becoming
thoughts outside my head

becoming sentences

written by

Jacqueline Amanda Woodson

SATURDAY MORNING

Some days in this new place
there is only a box of pancake mix
an egg, and faucet water, the hiss
of those together
against a black cast-iron pan,
the pancakes sticking to it
syrupless but edible and us
complaining about it wishing like anything
we were back in Greenville,
where there was always something good
to eat. We remember
the collards growing
down south, the melons, fresh picked
and dripping with a sweetness New York
can never know.
We eat without complaining
or whining or asking our mother when
   there will be
syrup, butter, milk . . .
We remember Greenville

without her, count our blessings in silence
and chew.

First Grade

My hand inside my sister's hand,
we walk the two blocks to P.S. 106 —
I am six years old and
my sister tells me our school was once a
  castle.
I believe her. The school stretches for a full
  city block.
Inside
marble stairs wind their way to classrooms
  filled
with dark wood desks
nailed down to dark wood floors polished
  to a high
and beautiful shine.

I am in love with everything around me,
the dotted white lines moving
across my teacher's blackboard, the smell
  of chalk,
the flag jutting out from the wall and
  slowly swaying

195

above me.

There is nothing more beautiful than P.S.
  106.
Nothing more perfect than my first-grade
  classroom.
No one more kind than Ms. Feidler, who
  meets me
at the door each morning,
takes my hand from my sister's, smiles
  down and says,
*Now that Jacqueline is here, the day can
  finally begin.*

And I believe her.
Yes, I truly believe her.

ANOTHER KINGDOM HALL

Because my grandmother calls and asks
if we're spreading Jehovah's word,
because my mother promises my
   grandmother
she'll raise us right in the eyes of God,
she finds a Kingdom Hall on Bushwick
   Avenue
so we can keep our Jehovah's Witness ways.
Every Sunday, we put on our Kingdom
   Hall clothes
pull out our Kingdom Hall satchels,
filled with our Kingdom Hall books
and walk the seven blocks
to the Kingdom Hall.

This is what reminds us of Greenville,
the Saturday-night pressing of satin ribbons,
Hope struggling with the knot in his tie,
our hair oiled and pulled back into braids,
our mother's hands less sure
than our grandmother's, the parts crooked,

the braids
coming undone. And now, Dell and I
are left to iron our own dresses.
My hands,
my mother says,
as she stands at the sink, holding a crying
    Roman
with one hand,
her other holding a bottle of milk
under hot running water,
are full.

My mother drops us off at the Kingdom
    Hall door,
watches us walk
down the aisle to where Brothers and
    Sisters
are waiting
to help us turn the pages of our Bibles,
lean over to share their songbooks with us,
press Life Savers into our waiting
    hands . . .

Then our mother is gone, back home
or to a park bench,
where she'll sit and read until the meeting
    is over.
She has a full-time job now. Sunday, she
    says,
is her day of rest.

FLAG

When the kids in my class ask why
I am not allowed to pledge to the flag
I tell them *It's against my religion* but don't
say,
I am in the world but not of the world. This,
they would not understand.
Even though my mother's not a Jehovah's
Witness,
she makes us follow their rules and
leave the classroom when the pledge is
being said.

Every morning, I walk out with Gina and
Alina
the two other Witnesses in my class.
Sometimes, Gina says,
Maybe we should pray for the kids inside
who don't know that God said
"No other idols before me." That our God
is a jealous God.
Gina is the true believer. Her Bible open

199

during reading time. But Alina and I walk
  through
our roles as Witnesses as though this is the
  part
we've been given in a play
and once offstage, we run free, sing
"America the Beautiful" and "The
  Star-Spangled Banner"
far away from our families — knowing
  every word.
Alina and I want
more than anything to walk back into our
  classroom
press our hands against our hearts. Say,
"I pledge allegiance . . ." loud
without our jealous God looking down on
  us.
  Without our parents finding out.
Without our mothers' voices
in our heads saying, *You are different.*
Chosen.
Good.

When the pledge is over, we walk single file
back into the classroom, take our separate
  seats
Alina and I far away from Gina. But Gina
always looks back at us — as if to say,
I'm watching you. As if to say,
I know.

We will never taste the sweetness of a
chosen
birthday cupcake.
We will never taste the bitterness of a
battle.

Because We're Witnesses

No Halloween.
No Christmas.
No birthdays.
Even when
other kids laugh as we leave the classroom
just as the birthday cupcakes arrive
we pretend we do not see the chocolate
   frosting,
pretend we do not want
to press our fingertips against
each colorful sprinkle and lift them,
one by sweet one
to our mouths.

No voting.
No fighting.
No cursing.
No wars.

We will never go to war.

We will never taste the sweetness of a
 classroom
birthday cupcake
We will never taste the bitterness of a
 battle.

BROOKLYN RAIN

The rain here is different than the way
it rains in Greenville. No sweet smell of
    honeysuckle.
No soft squish of pine. No slip and slide
    through grass.
Just Mama saying, *Stay inside today. It's
    raining,*
and me at the window. Nothing to do but
watch
the gray sidewalk grow darker,
watch
the drops slide down the glass pane,
watch
people below me move fast, heads bent.

Already there are stories
in my head. Already color and sound and
    words.
Already I'm
drawing circles on the glass, humming
myself someplace far away from here.

Down south, there was always someplace
   else to go
you could step out into the rain and
Grandma would let you
lift your head and stick out your tongue
be happy.

Down south already feels like a long time
   ago
but the stories in my head
take me back there, set me down in
   Daddy's garden
where the sun is always shining.

ANOTHER WAY

While our friends are watching TV or
   playing outside,
we are in our house, knowing that begging
   our mother
to turn the television on is useless, begging
   her for
ten minutes outside will only mean her
   saying,
No. Saying,
You can run wild with your friends anytime.
   Today
I want you to find another way to play.

And then one day my mother
comes home with two shopping bags
filled with board games — Monopoly,
   checkers, chess,
Ants in the Pants, Sorry, Trouble,
just about every game we've ever seen
in the commercials between
our Saturday morning cartoons.

205

So many games, we don't know
where to begin playing, so we let Roman
   choose.
And he chooses Trouble
because he likes the sound the die makes
when it pops inside
its plastic bubble. And for days and days,
it is Christmas in November,
games to play when our homework is done,
Monopoly money to count
and checkers to slam down on boards, ants
   to flip
into blue plastic pants,
chess pieces to practice moving until we
   understand
their power
and when we don't, Roman and I argue
that there's another way to play
called *Our Way.* But Hope and Dell tell us
that we're too immature to even begin to
   understand
then bend over the chessboard in silence,
   each becoming
the next chess champ of the house,
   depending on the day
and the way the game is played.

Sometimes, Roman and I leave Hope and
   Dell alone
go to another corner of the room and

become
what the others call us — *the two youngest,*
playing games we know the rules to
tic-tac-toe and checkers,
hangman and connect the dots

but mostly, we lean over their shoulders
as quietly as we can, watching
waiting
wanting to understand
how to play another way.

GIFTED

Everyone knows my sister
is brilliant. The letters come home folded
  neatly
inside official-looking envelopes that my
  sister proudly
hands over to my mother.
Odella has achieved
Odella has excelled at
Odella has been recommended to
Odella's outstanding performance in

She is gifted
we are told.
And I imagine presents surrounding her.

I am not gifted. When I read, the words
  twist
twirl across the page.
When they settle, it is too late.
The class has already moved on.

I want to catch words one day. I want to
   hold them
then blow gently,
watch them float
right out of my hands.

SOMETIMES

There is only one other house on our block
where a father doesn't live. When
    somebody asks why,
the boy says, *He died.*
The girl looks off, down the block, her
    thumb
slowly rising to her mouth. The boy says,
I was a baby. Says, *She doesn't remember
    him*
and points to his silent sister.

Sometimes, I lie about my father.
He died, I say, *in a car wreck* or
He fell off a roof or maybe
He's coming soon.
Next week and
next week and
next week . . . but
if my sister's nearby
she shakes her head. Says,
She's making up stories again.

Says,
We don't have a father anymore.
Says,
Our grandfather's our father now.
Says,
Sometimes, that's the way things happen.

UNCLE ROBERT

Uncle Robert has moved to New York City!

I hear him taking the stairs
two at a time and then
he is at our door, knocking loud until our
  mother
  opens it,
curlers in her hair, robe pulled closed,
  whispering,
*It's almost midnight, don't you wake my
children!*

But we are already awake, all four of us,
  smiling
  and jumping around
my uncle: *What'd you bring me?*

Our mama shushes us, says,
It's too late for presents and the like.
But we want presents and the like.
And she, too, is smiling now, happy to see

her baby brother who lives all the way
over
in Far Rockaway where the ocean is right
there
if you look out your window.

Robert opens his hand to reveal a pair of
silver earrings,
says to my sister, *This is a gift for how smart
you are.*
I want
to be smart like Dell, I want
someone to hand me silver and gold
just because my brain clicks into thinking
whenever
it needs to but
I am not smart like Dell so I watch her
press the silver moons into her ears
I say, *I know a girl ten times smarter than
her. She gets diamonds every time she
gets a hundred on a test.*
And Robert looks at me, his dark eyes
smiling, asks,
*Is that something you made up? Or
something real?*
In my own head,
it's real as anything.

In my head
all kinds of people are doing all kinds of
   things.
I want to tell him this, that
the world we're living in right here in
   Bushwick isn't
the only place. But now my brothers are
   asking,

What'd you bring me, and my uncle is
   pulling gifts
   from his pockets,
from his leather briefcase, from inside his
   socks.
   He hands
my mother a record, a small 45 — James
   Brown,
   who none of us
like because he screams when he sings. But
   my mother
   puts it on the record player, turned way
   down low
   and then even us kids are dancing
   around —
   Robert showing us the steps he learned
   at the Far Rockaway parties. His feet are
   magic
and we all try to slide across the floor like
   he does,
our own feet, again and again,

214

betraying us.

Teach us, Robert! we keep saying. *Teach us!*

WISHES

When he takes us to the park, Uncle
   Robert tells us,
If you catch a dandelion puff, you can make
   a wish.
Anything you want will come true, he says as
we chase the feathery wishes around
   swings,
beneath sliding boards,
until we can hold them in our hands,
close our eyes tight, whisper our dream
then set it floating out into the universe
   hoping
our uncle is telling the truth,
hoping each thing we wish for
will one day come true.

Believing

The stories start like this —

Jack and Jill went up a hill, my uncle sings.
I went up a hill yesterday, I say.
What hill?
In the park.
What park?
Halsey Park.
Who was with you?
Nobody.
*But you're not allowed to go to the park
  without anyone.*
I just did.
Maybe you dreamed it, my uncle says.
No, I really went.

And my uncle likes the stories I'm making
  up.

*. . . Along came a spider and sat down
  beside her.*

217

I got bit by a spider, I say.
When?
The other day.
Where?
Right on my foot.
Show us.
It's gone now.

But my mother accuses me of lying.
If you lie, she says, *one day you'll steal.*

I won't steal.
It's hard to understand how one leads to
   the other,
how stories could ever
make us criminals.

It's hard to understand
the way my brain works — so different
from everybody around me.
How each new story
I'm told becomes a thing
that happens,
in some other way
to me . . . !

Keep making up stories, my uncle says.
You're lying, my mother says.

Maybe the truth is somewhere in between

all that I'm told
and memory.

Off-Key

We start each meeting at Kingdom Hall
  with a song
and a prayer
but we're always late,
walking in when the pink songbooks are
  already open,
looking over shoulders, asking Brothers and
  Sisters
to help us find our place.
If it's a song I like, I sing loud until my
  sister shushes me
with a finger to her mouth.

My whole family knows I can't sing. My
  voice,
my sister says, is just left of the key. Just
  right
of the tune.

But I sing anyway, whenever I can.

Even the boring Witness songs sound good
   to me,
   the words
telling us how God wants us to behave,
what he wants us to do,
Be glad you nations with his people! Go
   preach
   from door to door!
The good news of Jehovah's kingdom —
Proclaim from shore to shore!

It's the music around the words that I hear
in my head, even though
everyone swears I *can't* hear it.
Strange that they don't hear
what I hear.

Strange that it sounds so right

to me.

EVE AND THE SNAKE

The Sunday sermons are given by men.
Women aren't allowed to get onstage like
    this,
standing alone to tell God's story. I don't
understand why but I listen anyway:

On the first day, God made the heavens and
    the earth
and He looked at it, and it was good.

It's a long story. It's a good story.
Adam and Eve got made,
a snake appeared in a tree. A talking snake.
Then Eve had to make a choice — the
    apple the snake
    wanted her to eat
looked so good — just one bite. But it was
    the only apple
    in a kingdom full of apples
that God had said *Don't touch!*

222

It's the best apple in all the world, the snake
   said.
   Go ahead and taste it. God won't care.

But we know the ending — in our heads,
   we scream,
*Don't do it, Eve! That's the Devil inside that
   snake!*
   He's tricking you!

But Eve took a bite. And so here we are,
sitting in a Kingdom Hall
on a beautiful Sunday afternoon
hoping that God sees it in His heart to
   know
it wasn't our fault. Give us another chance
send that snake back and we promise
we'll say no this time!

Our Father, Fading Away

In all our moving, we've forgotten our
    family in Ohio,
forgotten our father's voice, the slow drawl
of his words,
the way he and his brother David made
    jokes
that weren't funny
and laughed as though they were.

We forget the color of his skin — was it
dark brown like mine or lighter like Dell's?
Did he have Hope and Dell's loose curls or
    my
tighter, kinkier hair?

Was his voice deep or high?
Was he a hugger like Grandma Georgiana
    holding us
like she never planned to let go or
did he hug hard and fast like Mama,

planting her warm lips to our foreheads
    where
the kiss lingered
long after
she said I love you, pulled her sweater on
    and left
for work each morning.

In Brooklyn there are no more calls from
    Ohio.
No more calls from our father or Grandpa
    Hope
or Grandma Grace
or David or Anne or Ada or Alicia.

It is as if each family
has disappeared from the other.

Soon, someone who knows someone in
    Ohio
    who knows the Woodsons
tells my mother that Grandpa Hope has
    died.
At dinner that evening, our mother gives us
    the news but
we keep eating because we hadn't known
he was still alive.

And for a moment, I think about Jack . . .
    our father.

225

But then
quickly as it comes
the thought moves on.

Out of sight, out of mind, my brother says.

But only a part of me believes this is true.

Halfway Home #2

For a long time, there is only one tree on
  our block.
And though it still feels
strange to be so far away from soft dirt
beneath bare feet
the ground is firm here and the one tree
  blooms
wide enough to shade four buildings.
The city is settling around me, my words
  come fast now
when I speak, the soft curl of the South on
  my tongue
is near gone.

Who are these city children? My
  grandmother laughs,
her own voice
sad and far away on the phone. But it is
  a long-distance call
from Greenville to Brooklyn, too much
  money

and not enough time to explain
that New York City is gray rock
and quick-moving cars.
That the traffic lights change fast and my
  sister must
hold tight to my hand
as we cross to where a small man singing

Piragua! Piragua!
sells shaved ices from a white cart filled
with bottles and bottles of fruit-flavored
  syrup
colored red and purple, orange and blue.
That our mouths water in the hot sun as
  we hand him
our quarters then wait patiently as he
  pours
  the syrup over the ice, hands it to us
in paper cones.

We'll be coming home soon, Grandma
each of us promises.
We love you.

And when she says, *I love you, too*
the South is so heavy in her mouth
my eyes fill up with the missing of
everything and everyone
I've ever known.

THE PAINT EATER

In the night in the corner of the bedroom
the four of us share,
comes a pick, pick, picking of plaster
paint gone come morning.

My younger brother, Roman,
can't explain why paint melting
on his tongue feels good.

Still, he eats the paint
and plaster until a white hole
grows where pale green paint used to be.

And too late we catch him,
his fingers in his mouth,
his lips covered with dust.

CHEMISTRY

When Hope speaks, it's always about
  comic books
and superheroes
until my mother tells him he has to talk
about something else.
And then it's science. He wants to know
everything
about rockets and medicine and the galaxy.
He wants to know where the sky ends and
  how,
what does it feel like when gravity's gone
and what is the food men eat
on the moon. His questions come so fast
and so often that we forget how quiet
he once was until my mother
buys him a chemistry set.

And then for hours after school each day
he makes potions, mixing chemicals that
  stink up
the house, causing sparks to fly

from shaved bits of iron,
puffs of smoke to pop from strange-colored
  liquids.
We are fascinated by him, goggled and bent
  over the stove
a clamped test tube protruding
from his gloved hand.

On the days when our mother says
she doesn't want him smelling up the
  house
with his potions, he takes his trains apart,
  studies
each tiny piece, then slowly puts them
  together again.

We don't know what it is he's looking for
as he searches the insides of things, studies
the way things change. Each whispered
  Wow
from him makes me think that he
with his searching — and Dell with her
  reading
and even Roman with his trying to eat
to the other side of our walls — is looking
for something. Something way past
  Brooklyn.
Something
out
there.

BABY IN THE HOUSE

And then one day, Roman won't get up,
sun coming in bright
through the bedroom window, the rest of
  us
dressed and ready to go outside.
No laughter — just tears when we hold
  him.
More crying when we put him down.
Won't eat and even my mother
can't help him.

When she takes him to the hospital, she
  comes back

alone.

And for many days after that, there is no
  baby
in our house and I am finally
the baby girl again, wishing

I wasn't. Wishing there wasn't so much
  quiet
where my brother's laugh used to be,
  wishing

the true baby in our house
was home.

Going Home Again

July comes and Robert takes us on the
  night train
back to South Carolina. We kiss
our baby brother good-bye in his hospital
  bed where
he reaches out, cries to come with us.

His words are weak as water, no more
than a whisper with so much air around
  them.

I'm coming too, he says.

But he isn't coming.
Not this time.
My mother says there is lead in his blood
from the paint he finds a way to pick
and eat off our bedroom wall
every time our backs are turned.
Small holes grow, like white stars against
the green paint, covered again and again

by our mother. But still, he finds a way.
Each of us hugs him, promises
to bring him candy and toys.

Promises we won't have fun down south
without him.

Each of us leans in
for our mother's kiss on our forehead,
her warm lips, already a memory

that each of us carries home.

HOME AGAIN TO HALL STREET

My grandmother's kitchen is the same
big and yellow and smelling of the pound
  cake
she's made to welcome us back.

And now in the late afternoon, she is
  standing
at the sink, tearing collards beneath
cool running water, while the crows caw
  outside,
and the sun sinks slow into red and gold

When Hope lets the screen door slam,
she fusses,
Boy, don't you slam my door again! and my
  brother says,
I'm sorry.

Just like always.

Soon, there'll be lemonade on the porch,

the swing whining the same early evening
   song
it always sings
my brother and sister with the checker set
   between them
me next to my grandfather, falling asleep
   against
his thin shoulder.

And it's not even strange that it feels the
   way
   it's always felt
like the place we belong to.

Like *home*.

MRS. HUGHES'S HOUSE

In Greenville, my grandfather is too sick
to work anymore, so my grandmother has a
  full-time job.
Now we spend every day from July
until the middle of August
at Mrs. Hughes's Nursery and Day School.

Each morning, we walk the long dusty road
to Mrs. Hughes's house — large, white
  stone,
with a yard circling and chickens pecking
  at our feet.
Beyond the yard there's collards and corn
  growing
a scarecrow, black snakes, and
  whip-poor-wills.

She is a big woman, tall, yellow-skinned
  and thick
  as a wall.

I hold tight to my grandmother's hand.
  Maybe
I am crying.

My grandmother drops us off and
the other kids circle around us. Laughing
  at
our hair, our clothes, the names our
  parents
have given us,
our city way of talking — too fast, too
  many words
to hear at once
too many big words coming out of
my sister's mouth.

I am always the first to cry. A gentle slap
  on the side
of my head, a secret pinch,
girls circling around me singing, *Who stole*
  the cookie
from the cookie jar and
pointing, as though the song is true, at me.

My sister's tears are slow to come. But
  when they do,
it isn't sadness.
It's something different that sends her
  swinging
  her fists when

the others yank her braids until the satin,
newly ironed ribbons belong to them,
hidden away in the deep pockets of their
  dresses,
tucked into
their sagging stockings, buried inside their
silver lunch pails.

Hope is silent — his name, they say,
  belongs to a girl,
his ears, they laugh
stick out too far from his head.

Our feet are beginning to belong
in two different worlds — Greenville
and New York. We don't know how to
  come
home
and leave
home
behind us.

HOW TO LISTEN #4

Kids are mean, Dell says.
Just turn away. Pretend we
know better than that.

241

FIELD SERVICE

Saturday morning's the hardest day for us
  now.
For three hours we move through
the streets of Nicholtown,
knocking on strangers' doors, hoping to
  convert
them into Sisters and Brothers and
  children of God.

This summer I am allowed to knock on my
  first door
alone. An old woman answers, smiles
  kindly at me.
What a special child you are, she says.
Sky-blue ribbons in my hair, my
  Watchtower held tight
in my white-gloved hand,
the blue linen dress a friend of my
  grandmother's
has made for me stopping just above my
  knees.

My name is Jacqueline Woodson, I nearly
  whisper,
my throat suddenly dry
voice near gone.
*I'm here to bring you some good news
  today . . .*

Well how much does your good news cost,
  the woman
wants to know.

A dime.

She shakes her head sadly, closes her door
  a moment
to search beneath a trunk where she hopes
she's dropped a coin or two.
But when she comes back, there are no
  coins
in her hand.
Oh I'd love to read that magazine, she says.
I just don't have money.

And for many days my heart hurts with the
  sadness
that such a nice woman will not be a part
  of God's
new world.
It isn't fair, I say to my grandmother when
so many days have passed.

243

I want to go back. I want to give her
    something
    for free.

But we're done now with that strip of
    Nicholtown.
Next Saturday, we'll be somewhere else.
Another Witness will go there, my
    grandmother promises.
By and by, she says, *that woman will find her
    way.*

Sunday Afternoon
on the Front Porch

Across the road,
Miss Bell has tied a blue-checked
  sunbonnet
beneath her chin, lifts her head from her
  bed
of azaleas and waves to my grandmother.
I am sitting beside her on the front porch
  swing, Hope
and Dell leaning back against the wood
  beam
at the top of the front porch stairs. It is as
though we have always been in this
  position,
the front porch swing moving gently back
  and forth,
the sun warm on our faces, the day only
  halfway over.

I see your grands are back for the summer,
Miss Bell says. *Getting big, too.*

It is Sunday afternoon.

Out back, my grandfather pulls weeds from
  his garden,
digs softly into the rich earth to add new
  melon seeds.
  Wondering
if this time, they'll grow. All this he does
  from
a small chair, a cane beside him.
He moves as if underwater, coughs
hard and long into a handkerchief, calls
  out for Hope
when he needs the chair moved, sees me
  watching,
and shakes his head. *I'm catching you
  worrying,* he says.
*Too young for that. So just cut it out now, you
  hear?*
His voice
so strong and clear today, I can't help
  smiling.

Soon I'll rise from the porch,
change out of my Kingdom Hall clothes
  into
a pair of shorts and a cotton blouse
trade my patent-leather Mary Janes for
  bare feet
and join my grandfather in the garden.

What took you so long, he'll say. *I was about to turn*
this earth around without you.

Soon, it'll be near evening and Daddy and I
will walk slow
back into the house where I'll pull the
  Epsom salt
from the shelf
fill the dishpan with warm water, massage
his swelling hands.

But for now, I sit listening to Nicholtown
  settle
around me,
pray that one day Roman will be well
  enough
to know this moment.

Pray that we will always have this — the
  front porch,
my grandfather in the garden,
a woman in a blue-checked sunbonnet
moving through azaleas . . .

Pretty children, Miss Bell says.
But God don't make them no other kinda
  way.

HOME THEN HOME AGAIN

Too fast, our summer in Greenville
is ending.
Already, the phone calls from my mother
are filled with plans for coming home.
We miss
our little's brother's laughter, the way
he runs to us at the end of the school day
    as if
we've been gone forever. The way his small
    hands
curl around ours when we watch TV.
    Holding
tight through the scary parts, until we tell
    him
Scooby-Doo will save the day,
Bugs Bunny will get away,
Underdog will arrive before the train hits
Sweet Polly Purebred.

We drag our feet below our swings,

our arms wrapped lazily around the metal
   links
no longer fascinated by the newness
of the set, the way we climbed all over the
   slide,
pumped our legs hard — toward heaven
   until
the swing set shook with the weight of us
   lifting it
from the ground.

Next summer, my grandfather said, *I'll
   cement it down.*
But in the meantime
you all swing low.

Our suitcases sit at the foot of our bed,
   open
slowly filling with freshly washed summer
   clothes,
each blouse, each pair of shorts, each faded
   cotton dress
holding a story that we'll tell again and
   again
all winter long.

deep
in
my heart,
i do
believe

FAMILY

In the books, there's always a happily ever
    after.
The ugly duckling grows into a swan,
    Pinocchio
becomes a boy.
The witch gets chucked into the oven by
    Gretel,
the Selfish Giant goes to heaven.
Even Winnie the Pooh seems to always get
    his honey.
Little Red Riding Hood's grandmother is
    freed
from the belly of the wolf.

When my sister reads to me, I wait for the
    moment
when the story moves faster — toward the
    happy ending
that I know is coming.

On the bus home from Greenville, I wake

to the almost
happy ending, my mother standing at the
  station, Roman
in his stroller, his smile bright, his arms
  reaching for us
but we see the white hospital band like a
  bracelet
on his wrist. Tomorrow he will return
  there.

We are not all finally and safely
home.

ONE PLACE

For a long time, our little brother
goes back and forth to the hospital, his
  body
weak from the lead, his brain
not doing what a brain is supposed to do.
  We don't
understand why he's so small, has tubes
coming from his arms, sleeps and
  sleeps . . .
when we visit him.

But one day,
he comes home. The holes in the wall
are covered over and left
unpainted, his bed pulled away from
  temptation,
nothing for him to peel away.

He is four now, curls long gone, his dark
  brown hair
straight as a bone, strange to us but

our little brother, the four of us again

in one place.

MARIA

Late August now
home from Greenville and ready
for what the last of the summer brings me.
All the dreams this city holds
right outside — just step through the door
  and walk
two doors down to where
my new best friend, Maria, lives. Every
  morning,
I call up to her window, *Come outside*
or she rings our bell, *Come outside.*
Her hair is crazily curling down past her
  back,
the Spanish she speaks like a song
I am learning to sing.
Mi amiga, Maria.
Maria, my friend.

How to Listen #5

What is your one dream,
my friend Maria asks me.
Your one wish come true?

TOMBOY

My sister, Dell, reads and reads
and never learns
to jump rope or
play handball against the factory wall on
   the corner.
Never learns to sprint
barefoot down the block
to become
the fastest girl
on Madison Street.
Doesn't learn
to hide the belt or steal the bacon
or kick the can . . .
But I do and because of this
Tomboy becomes my new name.
My walk, my mother says,
reminds her of my father.
When I move long-legged and fast away
   from her
she remembers him.

GAME OVER

When my mother calls,
Hope Dell Jackie — inside!
the game is over.
No more reading beneath the streetlight
for Dell. But for my brother and me
it's no more *anything!* No more
steal the bacon
coco levio 1-2-3
Miss Lucy had a baby
spinning tops
double Dutch.
No more
freeze tag
hide the belt
hot peas and butter.
No more
singing contests on the stoop.
No more
ice cream truck chasing:
*Wait! Wait, ice cream man! My mother's
   gonna*

give me money!
No more getting wet in the johnny pump
or standing with two fisted hands out in
   front of me,
a dime hidden in one, chanting,
*Dumb school, dumb school, which hand's it
   in?*

When my mother calls,
Hope Dell Jackie — inside!
we complain as we walk up the block in
   the twilight:
*Everyone else is allowed to stay outside till
   dark.*
Our friends standing in the moment —
string halfway wrapped around a top,
waiting to be tagged and unfrozen,
searching for words to a song,
dripping from the johnny pump,
silent in the middle of *Miss Lucy had a . . .*

The game is over for the evening and all
   we can hear
is our friends'
Aw . . . man!!
Bummer!
For real?! This early?!
Dang it!
Shoot. Your mama's mean!
Early birds!

Why she gotta mess up our playing like that?
Jeez. Now
the game's over!

LESSONS

My mother says:

When Mama tried to teach me

to make collards and potato
salad I didn't want to learn.

She opens the box of pancake mix, adds
  milk
and egg, stirs. I watch
grateful for the food we have now — syrup
  waiting
in the cabinet, bananas to slice on top.
It's Saturday morning.
Five days a week, she leaves us
to work at an office back in Brownsville.
Saturday we have her to ourselves, all day
  long.

Me and Kay didn't want to be inside cooking.

She stirs the lumps from the batter, pours
  it
into the buttered, hissing pan.

Wanted to be with our friends
running wild through Greenville.

There was a man with a peach tree down the
  road.
One day Robert climbed over that fence,
  filled a bucket
with peaches. Wouldn't share them with any
  of us but
told us where the peach tree was. And that's
  where we
wanted to be
sneaking peaches from that man's tree,
  throwing
the rotten ones
at your uncle!

Mama wanted us to learn to cook.

Ask the boys, we said. And Mama knew that
  wasn't fair
girls inside and boys going off to steal
  peaches!
So she let all of us
stay outside until suppertime.

And by then, she says, putting our breakfast

on the table,

it was too late.

TRADING PLACES

When Maria's mother makes
arroz con habichuelas y tostones,
we trade dinners. If it's a school night,
I'll run to Maria's house, a plate of my
    mother's
baked chicken with Kraft mac and cheese,
sometimes box corn bread,
sometimes canned string beans,
warm in my hands, ready for the first taste
of Maria's mother's garlicky rice and
    beans,
crushed green bananas
fried and salted and warm . . .

Maria will be waiting, her own plate
    covered in foil.
    Sometimes
we sit side by side on her stoop, our traded
    plates
in our laps.
What are you guys eating? the

neighborhood kids ask
but we never answer, too busy shoveling
  the food we love
into our mouths.
Your mother makes the best chicken, Maria
  says. *The best corn bread. The best
  everything!*
Yeah, I say.
*I guess my grandma taught her something
  after all.*

WRITING #1

It's easier to make up stories
than it is to write them down. When I
  speak,
the words come pouring out of me. The
  story
wakes up and walks all over the room. Sits
  in a chair,
crosses one leg over the other, says,
Let me introduce myself. Then just starts
  going on and on.
But as I bend over my composition
  notebook,
only my name
comes quickly. Each letter, neatly printed
between the pale blue lines. Then white
space and air and me wondering, *How do I
spell introduce?* Trying again and again
until there is nothing but pink
bits of eraser and a hole now
where a story should be.

Late Autumn

Ms. Moskowitz calls us one by one and
  says,
Come up to the board and write your name.
When it's my turn, I walk down the aisle
  from
my seat in the back, write *Jacqueline*
  Woodson —
the way I've done a hundred times, turn
  back
toward my seat, proud as anything
of my name in white letters on the dusty
  blackboard.
But Ms. Moskowitz stops me, says,
In cursive too, please. But the *q* in
  Jacqueline is too hard
so I write *Jackie Woodson* for the first
  time. Struggle
only a little bit with the *k*.

Is that what you want us to call you?

I want to say, *No, my name is Jacqueline*

but I am scared of that cursive *q*, know
I may never be able to connect it to *c* and
   u
so I nod even though
I am lying.

THE OTHER WOODSON

Even though so many people think my
  sister and I
are twins,
I am the other Woodson, following behind
  her each year
into the same classroom she had the year
  before. Each
teacher smiles when they call my name.
  Woodson, they
say. *You must be Odella's sister.* Then they
  nod
slowly, over and over again, call me Odella.
  Say,
*I'm sorry! You look so much like her and she
  is SO brilliant!*
then wait for my brilliance to light up
the classroom. Wait for my arm to fly into
the air with every answer. Wait for my
  pencil
to move quickly through the too-easy math
  problems

on the mimeographed sheet. Wait for me to stand
before class, easily reading words even high school
students stumble over. And they keep waiting.
And waiting
and waiting
and waiting

until one day, they walk into the classroom,
almost call me Odel — then stop

remember that I am the other Woodson

and begin searching for brilliance

at another desk.

WRITING #2

On the radio, Sly and the Family Stone are
  singing
"Family Affair," the song turned up
  because it's
my mother's favorite, the one she plays
  again and again.

You can't leave 'cause your heart is there,
  Sly sings.
But you can't stay 'cause you been
  somewhere else.

The song makes me think of Greenville
  and Brooklyn
the two worlds my heart lives in now. I am
  writing
the lyrics down, trying to catch each word
  before it's gone

then reading them back, out loud to my
  mother. This

is how I'm learning. Words come slow to
    me
on the page until
I memorize them, reading the same books
    over
and over, copying
lyrics to songs from records and TV
    commercials,
the words
settling into my brain, into my memory.
Not everyone learns
to read this way — memory taking over
    when the rest
of the brain stops working,
but I do.

Sly is singing the words
over and over as though
he is trying
to convince me that this whole world
is just a bunch of families
like ours

going about their own family affairs.

Stop daydreaming, my mother says.

So I go back to writing down words
that are songs and stories and whole new
    worlds

tucking themselves into
my memory.

BIRCH TREE POEM

Before my teacher reads the poem,
she has to explain.
A birch, she says, *is a kind of tree*
then magically she pulls a picture
from her desk drawer and the tree is
  suddenly
real to us.

"When I see birches bend to left and
  right . . ." she begins
"Across the lines of straighter darker trees,
I like to think" —

and when she reads, her voice drops down
  so low
and beautiful
some of us put our heads on our desks to
  keep
the happy tears from flowing

— *"some boy's been swinging them.*
But swinging doesn't bend them down to stay

As ice-storms do."

And even though we've never seen an ice
   storm
we've seen a birch tree, so we can imagine
everything we need to imagine

forever and ever

infinity

amen.

How to Listen #6

When I sit beneath
the shade of my block's oak tree
the world disappears.

READING

I am not my sister.
Words from the books curl around each
  other
make little sense
until
I read them again
and again, the story
settling into memory. *Too slow*
the teacher says.
Read faster.
Too babyish, the teacher says.
Read older.
But I don't want to read faster or older or
any way else that might
make the story disappear too quickly from
  where
  it's settling
inside my brain,
slowly becoming
a part of me.
A story I will remember

long after I've read it for the second, third, tenth, hundredth time.

STEVIE AND ME

Every Monday, my mother takes us
to the library around the corner. We are
  allowed
to take out seven books each. On those
  days,
no one complains
that all I want are picture books.

Those days, no one tells me to read faster
to read harder books
to read like Dell.

No one is there to say, *Not that book,*
when I stop in front of the small paperback
with a brown boy on the cover.
Stevie.

I read:
One day my momma told me,
"You know you're gonna have
a little friend come stay with you."

And I said, "Who is it?"

If someone had been fussing with me
to read like my sister, I might have missed
the picture book filled with brown people,
 more
brown people than I'd ever seen
in a book before.

The little boy's name was Steven but
his mother kept calling him Stevie.
My name is Robert but my momma don't
call me Robertie.

If someone had taken
that book out of my hand
said, *You're too old for this*
maybe
I'd never have believed
that someone who looked like me
could be in the pages of the book
that someone who looked like me
had a story.

WHEN I TELL MY FAMILY

When I tell my family
I want to be a writer, they smile and say,
We see you in the backyard with your writing.
They say,
We hear you making up all those stories.
And,
We used to write poems.
And,
*It's a good hobby, we see how quiet it keeps
    you.*
They say,
But maybe you should be a teacher,
a lawyer,
do hair . . .

I'll think about it, I say.

And maybe all of us know

this is just another one of my
stories.

283

DADDY GUNNAR

Saturday morning and Daddy Gunnar's
  voice
is on the other end of the phone.
We all grab for it.
Let me speak to him!
My turn!
No mine!
Until Mama makes us stand in line.

He coughs hard, takes deep breaths.
When he speaks, it's almost low as a
  whisper.

How are my New York grandbabies, he
  wants to know.

We're good, I say, holding tight to the
  phone
but my sister is already grabbing for it,
Hope and even Roman, all of us
hungry for the sound
of his faraway voice.

284

Y'all know how much I love you?

Infinity and back again, I say
the way I've said it a million times.

And then, Daddy says to me, *Go on and add*
a little bit more to that.

HOPE ONSTAGE

Until the curtain comes up and he's
  standing there,
ten years old and alone in the center of the
  P.S. 106 stage,
no one knew
my big brother could sing. He is dressed
  as a shepherd, his voice
soft and low, more sure than any sound
  I've ever heard
come out of him. My quiet big brother
  who only speaks
when asked, has little to say to any of us,
  except
when he's talking about science or comic
  books, now
has a voice that is circling the air,
landing clear and sweet around us:

"Tingalayo, come little donkey come.
Tingalayo, come little donkey come.
My donkey walks, my donkey talks

my donkey eats with a knife and fork.
Oh Tingalayo, come little donkey come."

Hope can sing . . . my sister says in wonder
 as my mother
and the rest of the audience start to clap.

Maybe, I am thinking, there is something
 hidden
like this, in all of us. A small gift from the
 universe
waiting to be discovered.

My big brother raises his arms, calling his
 donkey home.
He is smiling as he sings, the music getting
 louder
behind him.

"Tingalayo . . ."

And in the darkened auditorium, the light
is only on Hope
and it's hard to believe he has such a
 magic singing voice
and even harder to believe his donkey
is going to come running.

DADDY THIS TIME

Greenville is different this summer,

Roman is well and out back, swinging
   hard. Somewhere
between last summer and now, our daddy
cemented the swing set down.
Roman doesn't know the shaky days —
   just this moment,
his dark blue Keds pointing toward the sky,
   his laughter and screams, like wind
through the screen door.
Now my grandmother shushes him,
Daddy resting in the bedroom, the covers
   pulled up to his chin,
his thin body so much smaller than I
   remember it.

Just a little tired, Daddy says to me, when I
   tiptoe
in with chicken soup,

sit on the edge of the bed and try to get
   him
to take small sips.
He struggles into sitting, lets me feed him
small mouthfuls but only a few
are enough. *Too tired to eat anymore.*
Then he closes his eyes.

Outside, Roman laughs again and the
   swing set
whines with the weight of him.
Maybe Hope is there, pushing him
into the air. Or maybe it's Dell.
The three of them would rather be outside.

His room smells, my sister says.
But I don't smell anything except the
   lotion
I rub into my grandfather's hands.
When the others aren't around, he
   whispers,
   You're my favorite,
smiles and winks at me. *You're going to be
   fine,*
   you know that.
Then he coughs hard and closes his eyes,
   his breath
struggling to get
into and out of his body.

Most days, I am in here with my
   grandfather,
      holding his hand
while he sleeps
fluffing pillows and telling him stories
about my friends back home.
When he asks, I speak to him in Spanish,
the language that rolls off my tongue
like I was born knowing it.
Sometimes, my grandfather says,
Sing me something pretty.

And when I sing to him, I'm not
just left of the key or right of the tune
He says I sing beautifully.

He says I am perfect.

WHAT EVERYBODY KNOWS NOW

Even though the laws have changed
my grandmother still takes us
to the back of the bus when we go
   downtown
in the rain. *It's easier,* my grandmother
   says,
*than having white folks look at me like I'm
   dirt.*

But we aren't dirt. We are people
paying the same fare as other people.
When I say this to my grandmother,
she nods, says, *Easier to stay where you
   belong.*

I look around and see the ones
who walk straight to the back. See
the ones who take a seat up front, daring
anyone to make them move. And know
this is who I want to be. Not scared
like that. Brave

like that.

Still, my grandmother takes my hand
    downtown
pulls me right past the restaurants that
    have to let us sit
wherever we want now. *No need in making
    trouble,*
she says. *You all go back to New York City
    but
I have to live here.*

We walk straight past Woolworth's
without even looking in the windows
because the one time my grandmother
    went inside
they made her wait and wait. *Acted like
I wasn't even there.* It's hard *not* to see the
    moment —
my grandmother in her Sunday clothes, a
    hat
with a flower pinned to it
neatly on her head, her patent-leather
    purse,
perfectly clasped
between her gloved hands — waiting
    quietly
long past her turn.

END OF SUMMER

Too fast the summer leaves us, we kiss
our grandparents good-bye and my uncle
  Robert
is there waiting
to take us home again.

When we hug our grandfather, his body
is all bones and skin. But he is up now,
sitting at the window, a blanket covering
his thin shoulders.

Soon, I'll get back to that garden, he says.
But most days, all I want to do
is lay down and rest.

We wave again from the taxi that pulls out
slow down the drive — watch our
  grandmother,
still waving,
grow small behind us and our grandfather,

in the window,
fade from sight.

FAR ROCKAWAY

Robert only stays long enough
for my mother to thank him
for buying our tickets
for getting us home.

He does a fancy turn on his heel, aims
two pointer fingers at us
says, *I'll catch up with all of you later.*

We tell him that he has to come back soon,
remind him of all the stuff he's promised
  us
trips to Coney Island and Palisades
  Amusement Park,
  a Crissy doll
with hair that grows, a Tonka toy, *Gulliver's
  Travels,*
  candy.

He says he won't forget,
asks us if he's a man of his word and

everyone except my mother
nods.

Hard not to miss my mother's eyebrows,
giving her baby brother a look,
pressing her lips together. Once,
in the middle of the night, two policemen
knocked on our door, asking for Robert
  Leon Irby.
But my uncle wasn't here.

So now my mother takes a breath, says,
Stay safe.
Says,
Don't get into trouble out there, Robert.

He gives her a hug, promises he won't
and then he is gone.

FRESH AIR

When I get back to Brooklyn, Maria isn't
    there.
She's gone upstate, staying with a family,
her mother tells me, that has a pool. Then
    her mother
puts a plate of food in front of me, tells me
how much she knows I love her rice and
    chicken.

When Maria returns she is tanned and
    wearing
a new short set. Everything about her
    seems different.
I stayed with white people, she tells me. *Rich
    white people.*
*The air upstate is different. It doesn't smell
    like anything!*
She hands me a piece of bubble gum with
    BUBBLE YUM
in bright letters.
This is what they chew up there.

297

The town was called Schenectady.

All the rest of the summer Maria and I buy
   only Bubble Yum, blow
huge bubbles while I make her tell me
   story after
story about the white family in
   Schenectady.

*They kept saying I was poor and trying to
   give me stuff,*
Maria says. *I had to keep telling them it's not
   poor*
where we live.
Next summer, I say. *You should just come
   down south.*
It's different there.

And Maria promises she will.

On the sidewalk we draw hopscotch games
   that we
play using chipped pieces of slate, chalk
Maria & Jackie Best Friends Forever
   wherever
there is smooth stone.
Write it so many times that it's hard to
   walk
on our side
of the street without looking down

and seeing us there.

P.S. 106 HAIKU

Jacqueline Woodson.
I'm finally in fourth grade.
It's raining outside.

LEARNING FROM LANGSTON

I loved my friend.

He went away from me.
There's nothing more to say.
The poem ends,
Soft as it began —
I loved my friend.

— Langston Hughes

I love my friend
and still do
when we play games
we laugh. I hope she never goes away from
*   me*
because I love my friend.

— Jackie Woodson

The Selfish Giant

In the story of the Selfish Giant, a little
  boy hugs
a giant who has never been hugged before.
The giant falls
in love with the boy but then one day,
the boy disappears.
When he returns, he has scars on his hands
  and
his feet, just like Jesus.
The giant dies and goes to Paradise.

The first time my teacher reads the story
  to the class
I cry all afternoon, and am still crying
when my mother gets home from work that
  evening.

She doesn't understand why
I want to hear such a sad story again and
  again

but takes me to the library around the
   corner
when I beg
and helps me find the book to borrow.
The Selfish Giant, by Oscar Wilde.

I read the story again and again.
Like the giant, I, too, fall in love with the
   Jesus boy,
there's something so sweet about him, I
   want
to be his friend.

Then one day, my teacher asks me to come
   up front
to read out loud. But I don't need to bring
the book with me.
The story of the Selfish Giant is in my
   head now,
living there. Remembered.

*"Every afternoon, as they were coming from
   school,*
*the children used to go and play in the
   Giant's garden . . ."*
I tell the class, the whole story flowing out
   of me
right up to the end when the boy says,

"These are the wounds of Love . . .
"You let me play once in your garden, today

*you shall
come with me to my garden, which is
Paradise . . ."*

How did you do that, my classmates ask.
How did you memorize all those words?

But I just shrug, not knowing what to say.
How can I explain to anyone that stories
are like air to me,
I breathe them in and let them out
over and over again.

Brilliant! my teacher says, smiling.
Jackie, that was absolutely beautiful.

And I know now
words are my Tingalayo. Words are my
  brilliance.

THE BUTTERFLY POEMS

No one believes me when I tell them
I am writing a book about butterflies,
even though they see me with the *Childcraft*
  encyclopedia
heavy on my lap opened to the pages
  where
the monarch, painted lady, giant
  swallowtail and
queen butterflies live. Even one called a
  buckeye.

When I write the first words
Wings of a butterfly whisper . . .

no one believes a whole book could ever
  come
from something as simple as
butterflies that *don't even,* my brother says,
live that long.

But on paper, things can live forever.

On paper, a butterfly
never dies.

Six Minutes

The Sisters in the Kingdom Hall get six
  minutes
to be onstage. In pairs. Or threes.
But never alone.
We have to write skits
where we are visiting another Sister
or maybe a nonbeliever. Sometimes
the play takes place at their pretend
  kitchen table
and sometimes, we're in their pretend
  living room
but in real life we're just in folding chairs,
  sitting
on the Kingdom Hall stage. The first time
I have to give my talk I ask if I can write it
  myself
without anyone helping.
There are horses and cows in my story
  even though
the main point is supposed to be
the story of the resurrection.

307

Say for instance, I write,
we have a cow and a horse that we love.
Is death the end of life for those animals?
When my mother reads those lines,
she shakes her head. *You're getting away*
  from the topic,
she says. *You have to take the animals out of*
  it, get right
to the point. Start with people.
I don't know what I am supposed to do
with the fabulous, more interesting part of
  my story,
where the horses and cows start speaking
  to me
and to each other. How even though they
  are old
and won't live much longer, they aren't
  afraid.
You only have six minutes, my mother says,
and no, you can't get up and walk across the
  stage
to make your point. Your talk has to be given
sitting down.

So I start again. Rewriting:
Good afternoon, Sister. I'm here to bring you
  some
good news today.
Did you know God's word is absolute? If we
  turn to John,

promising myself there'll come a time
when I can use the rest of my story
and stand when I tell it
and give myself and my horses and my
  cows
a whole lot more time
than six minutes!

First Book

There are seven of them,
haikus mostly but rhyming ones, too.
Not enough for a real book until
I cut each page into a small square
staple the squares together, write
one poem
on each page.
Butterflies by Jacqueline Woodson
on the front.

The butterfly book
complete now.

JOHN'S BARGAIN STORE

Down Knickerbocker Avenue is where
  everyone
on the block goes to shop.
There's a pizzeria if you get hungry,
seventy-five cents a slice.
There's an ice cream shop where cones
  cost a quarter.
There's a Fabco Shoes store and a beauty
  parlor.
A Woolworth's five-and-dime and a John's
  Bargain Store.
For a long time, I don't put one foot inside
  Woolworth's.
*They wouldn't let Black people eat at their
  lunch counters*
in Greenville, I tell Maria.
No way are they getting my money!
So instead, Maria and I go to John's
  Bargain Store where
three T-shirts cost a dollar. We buy them

in pale pink, yellow and baby blue. Each night
   we make a plan:
Wear your yellow one tomorrow, Maria says,
and I'll wear mine.
All year long, we dress alike,
walking up and down Madison Street
waiting for someone to say, *Are you guys*
   cousins?
so we can smile, say,
Can't you tell from looking at us?!

New Girl

Then one day a new girl moves in next
 door, tells us
her name is Diana and becomes
me and Maria's Second Best Friend in the
 Whole World.
And even though Maria's mother
knew Diana's mother in Puerto Rico,
Maria promises that doesn't make Diana
 más mejor
amiga — a better friend. But some days,
 when
it's raining and Mama won't let me go
 outside,
I see them
on the block, their fingers laced together,
heading around the corner
to the bodega for candy. Those days,
the world feels as gray and cold as it really
 is
and it's hard
not to believe the new girl isn't *más mejor*

than me.
Hard not to believe
my days as Maria's best friend forever and
  ever amen
are counted.

PASTELES & PERNIL

When Maria's brother, Carlos, gets
    baptized
he is just a tiny baby in a white lace gown
    with
so many twenty-dollar bills folded into fans
    pinned
all over it
that he looks like a green-and-white angel.

Maria and I stand over his crib
talking about all the candy we could buy
    with just one
of those fans. But we know that God is
    watching
and don't even dare touch the money.

In the kitchen, there is *pernil* roasting in
    the oven
the delicious smell filling the house and
    Maria says,

You should just eat a little bit. But I am not
    allowed
to eat pork. Instead, I wait for *pasteles* to
    get
passed around,
wait for the ones her mother has filled with
    chicken
for Jackie, mi ahijada, wait for the moment
    when
I can peel the paper
away from the crushed-plantain-covered
    meat,
break off small pieces with my hands and
    let the
pastele melt in my mouth. *My mother
    makes the best
pasteles in Brooklyn,* Maria says. And even
    though I've
only eaten her mom's, I agree.

Whenever there is the smell of *pernil* and
    pasteles on
the block, we know
there is a celebration going on. And
    tonight, the party
is at Maria's house. The music is loud and
    the cake
is big and the *pasteles*
that her mother's been making for three
    days are

absolutely perfect.

We take our food out to her stoop just as
   the grown-ups
start dancing merengue, the women lifting
   their long dresses
to show off their fast-moving feet,
the men clapping and yelling,
Baila! Baila! until the living room floor
   disappears.
When I ask Maria where Diana is she says,
*They're coming later. This part is just for my
   family.*

She pulls the crisp skin
away from the *pernil,* eats the pork
   shoulder
with rice and beans,
our plates balanced on our laps, tall glasses
   of Malta
beside us.
and for a long time, neither one of us says
   anything.

Yeah, I say. *This is only for us. The family.*

CURSES

We are good kids,
people tell my mother this all the time, say,
You have the most polite children.
I've never heard a bad word from them.

And it's true — we say *please* and *thank
you.*
We speak softly. We look adults in the eyes
ask, *How are you?* Bow our heads when we
pray.
We don't know how to curse,
when we try to put bad words together
they sound strange
like new babies trying to talk and mixing
up their sounds.

At home, we aren't allowed words like
stupid or *dumb* or *jerk* or *darn.*
We aren't allowed to say
I hate or *I could die* or *You make me sick.*

318

We're not allowed to roll our eyes or
look away when my mother is speaking to
    us.

Once my brother said *butt* and wasn't
    allowed
to play outside after school for a week.
When we are with our friends and angry,
    we whisper,
You stupid dummy
and our friends laugh then spew curses
at us like bullets, bend their lips over the
    words
like they were born speaking them. They
    coach us on,
tell us to *Just say it!*

But we can't. Even when we try
the words get caught inside our throats, as
    though
our mother
is standing there waiting, daring them to
    reach the air.

AFROS

When Robert comes over with his hair
  blown out into
an afro, I beg my mother
for the same hairstyle.
Everyone in the neighborhood
has one and all of the black people on *Soul
  Train.* Even
Michael Jackson and his brothers are all
  allowed to wear
their hair this way.
Even though she says no to me,
my mom spends a lot of Saturday morning
in her bedroom mirror,
picking her own hair
into a huge black and beautiful dome.
Which
is so completely one hundred percent
  unfair
but she says, *This is the difference between
being a grown-up and being a child.* When
she's not looking, I stick my tongue out

at her.
My sister catches me, says,
And that's the difference
between being a child and being a grown-up,
like she's twenty years old.
Then rolls her eyes at me and goes back to
   reading.

GRAFFITI

Your tag is your name written with spray
  paint
however you want it wherever you want it
  to be.
It doesn't even have to be
your real name — like Loco who lives on
  Woodbine Street.
His real name is Orlando but everyone
calls him by his tag so
it's everywhere in Bushwick. Black and red
  letters and
crazy eyes inside the Os.
Some kids climb to the tops of buildings,
  hang
over the edge
spray their names upside down from there.

But me and Maria only know the ground,
  only know
the factory on the corner with its newly
  painted

bright pink wall. Only know the way my
  heart jumps
as I press the button down, hear the hiss of
  paint, watch
J-A-C-begin.

Only know the sound of my uncle's voice,

stopping me before my name is
a part of the history — like the ones on the
  roofs
and fire escapes and subway cars. I wish
I could explain.
Wish I had the words
to stop his anger, stop the force of him
  grabbing my hand,
wish I knew how to say,
Just let me write — everywhere!

But my uncle keeps asking over and over
  again,

What's wrong with you?
Have you lost your mind?
Don't you know people get arrested
for this?

They're just words, I whisper.
They're not trying to hurt anybody!

MUSIC

Each morning the radio comes on at seven
  o'clock.
Sometimes Michael Jackson is singing that
  A-B-C
is as easy as 1-2-3
or Sly and the Family Stone are thanking
  us for
letting them
be themselves.
Sometimes it's slower music, the Five
  Stairsteps
telling us
things are going to get easier, or the Hollies
  singing,
He ain't heavy, he's my brother
So on we go . . .

My mother lets us choose what music we
  want
to listen to
as long as the word *funk* doesn't appear

anywhere
in the song.
But the summer I am ten, *funk* is in every
   single song
that comes on the cool black radio stations.
   So our
mother makes us listen
to the white ones.

All afternoon corny people sing about
   Colorado,
about everything being beautiful
about how we've only just begun.
My sister falls in love
with the singers but I sneak off
to Maria's house where
safe inside her room with the pink shag
   carpet
and bunk beds,
we can comb our dolls' hair and sing along
   when
the Ohio Players say,
He's the funkiest
Worm in the world.
We can dance
the Funky Chicken, tell imaginary
   intruders
to get the funk out
of our faces. Say the word so hard and so
   loud

and so many times,
it becomes something different to us —
   something
   so silly
we laugh just thinking about it.
Funky, funky, funky,
we sing again and again until the word is
   just a sound
not connected to anything
good or bad
right or wrong.

RIKERS ISLAND

When the phone call comes in the middle
  of the night,
    it isn't
to tell us someone has died. It's Robert
calling from a prison called Rikers Island.
Even from my half-asleep place,
I can hear my mother taking a heavy
  breath, whispering,
I knew this was coming, Robert. I knew you
  weren't
doing right.

In the morning, we eat our cereal in silence
  as our mother tells us
that our uncle won't be around for a while.
When we ask where he's gone, she says,
  Jail.
When we ask why, she says,
It doesn't matter. We love him.
That's all we need to know and keep
  remembering.

Robert walked the wide road, she says. *And now*
he's paying for it.

Witnesses believe there's a wide road and a
  narrow road.
To be good in the eyes of God is to walk
  the narrow one,
live a good clean life, pray, do what's right.
On the wide road, there is every kind of
  bad thing anyone
can imagine. I imagine my uncle doing his
  smooth
dance steps down the wide road,
smiling as the music plays loud. I imagine
him laughing, pressing quarters into our
  palms,
pulling presents for us from his bag, thick
  gold
bracelet flashing at his wrist.
Where'd you get this? my mother asked, her
  face tight.
It doesn't matter, my uncle answered. *Y'all*
  know I love you.

You doing the right thing, Robert? my
mother wanted
to know. *Yes,* my uncle said. *I promise you.*

It rains all day. We sit around the house

328

waiting for the sun to come out so we can
  go outside.
Dell reads in the corner of our room. I pull
  out
my beat-up composition notebook
try to write another butterfly poem.
Nothing comes.

The page looks like the day — wrinkled
  and
empty no longer promising anyone
anything.

Moving Upstate

From Rikers Island, my uncle is sent
to a prison upstate we can visit.

We don't know what he'll look like, how
much he'll have changed. And because our
  mother
warns us not to, I don't tell anyone he's in
  jail.

When my friends ask, I say, *He moved
  upstate.*
We're going to visit him soon.

He lives in a big house, I say. *With a big
  yard and everything.*

But the missing settles inside of me. Every
  time
James Brown comes on the radio, I see
  Robert dancing.

Every time the commercial for the Crissy

doll comes on
I think how I almost got one.

He's my favorite uncle, I say one afternoon.

He's our ONLY uncle, my sister says.
Then goes back to reading.

ON THE BUS
TO DANNEMORA

We board the bus when the sun is just
  kissing the sky.
Darkness like a cape that we wear for
  hours, curled into it
and back to sleep. From somewhere above
  us
the O'Jays are singing, telling people all
  over the world
to join hands and start a love train.
The song rocks me gently into and out of
  dreaming
and in the dream, a train filled with love
  goes on and on.

And in the story that begins from the song,
  the bus
is no longer a bus and we're no longer
  going to
Dannemora. But there is food and laughter
  and

the music. The girl telling the story is me
  but
not me at the same time — watching all of
  this,
writing it down as fast as she can,
singing along with the O'Jays, asking
  everyone
to let this train keep on riding . . .
"riding on through . . ."

and it's the story of a whole train filled
with love and how the people on it
aren't in prison but are free to dance
and sing and hug their families whenever
  they want.

On the bus, some of the people are
  sleeping, others
are staring out the window or talking softly.
Even the children are quiet. Maybe each of
  them
  is thinking
their own dream — of daddies and uncles,
  brothers
  and cousins
one day being free to come on board.

Please don't miss this train at the station
'Cause if you miss it, I feel sorry, sorry for
  you.

Too Good

The bus moves slow out of the city until
  we can see
the mountains, and above that, so much
  blue sky.

Passing the mountains.

Passing the sea
Passing the heavens.
That's soon where I will be . . .

A song comes to me quickly, the words
  moving through
my brain and out of my mouth in a
  whisper but still
my sister hears, asks who taught it to me.

I just made it up, I say.

No you didn't, she says back. *It's too good.*
  Someone
taught that to you.

I don't say anything back. Just look out the
   window
and smile.

Too good, I am thinking. The stuff I make
   up is *too good.*

DANNEMORA

At the gate of the prison, guards glare at
  us, then slowly
allow us in.

My big brother is afraid.
He looks up at the barbed wire
puts his hands in his pockets.
I know he wishes he was home with his
  chemistry set.
I know he wants to be anywhere but here.
Nothing but stone and a big building that
  goes so far up
and so far back and forth that we can't see
where the beginning is
or where it might end. Gray brick, small
  windows
covered with wire. Who could see
out from here? The guards check our
  pockets,
check our bags, make us
walk through X-ray machines.

My big brother holds out his arms. Lets
  the guards pat him
from shoulder to ankle, checking
for anything he might be hiding . . .
He is Hope Austin Woodson the Second,
  part of a long line
of Woodsons — doctors and lawyers and
  teachers —
but as quickly as THAT! he can become
a number. Like Robert Leon Irby is now
so many numbers across the pocket
of his prison uniform that it's hard
not to keep looking at them,
waiting for them to morph into letters
that spell out
my uncle's name.

Not Robert

When the guard brings our uncle to the
  waiting room
that is filled with other families
waiting, he is not
Robert. His afro is gone now,
shaved to a black shadow on his perfect
  skull.
His eyebrows are thicker than I remember,
  dipping down
in a newer, sadder way. Even when he
  smiles,
opens his arms
to hug all of us at once, the bit I catch of
  it, before
jumping into his hug, is a half smile,
  caught
and trapped inside a newer, sadder
uncle.

MOUNTAIN SONG

On the way home from visiting Robert,
I watch the mountains move past me
and slowly the mountain song starts
  coming again
more words this time, coming faster
than I can sing them.

Passing the mountains
Passing the sea
Passing the heavens
waiting for me.

Look at the mountains
Such a beautiful sea
And there's a promise that heaven
is filled with glory.

I sing the song over and over again,
quietly into the windowpane, my forehead
pressed against the cool glass. Tears coming
  fast now.

The song makes me think of Robert and
    Daddy
    and Greenville
and everything that feels far behind me
    now, everything
that is going

or already gone.

I am thinking if I can hold on to the
    memory of this song
get home and write it down, then it will
    happen,
I'll be a writer. I'll be able to hold on to
each moment, each memory
everything.

POEM ON PAPER

When anyone in the family asks
what I'm writing, I usually say,
Nothing
or
A story
or
A poem
and only my mother says,
Just so long as you're not writing about our
* family.*

And I'm not.

Well, not really . . .

Up in the mountains
far from the sea
there's a place called Dannemora
the men are not free . . .

341

DADDY

It is early spring
when my grandmother sends for us.

Warm enough to believe again
that food will come from the newly thawed
  earth.
This is the weather, my mother says, *Daddy
  loved
to garden in.* We arrive
not long before my grandfather is about to
  take
his last breaths,
breathless ourselves from our first ride
in an airplane.

I want to tell him all about it
how loud it was when the plane lifted into
  the sky,
each of us, leaning toward the window,
watching New York
grow small and speckled beneath us.

How the meals arrived
on tiny trays — some kind of fish that none
  of us ate.
I want to tell him how the stewardess gave
  us wings
to pin to our blouses and shirts and told
  Mama
we were beautiful and well behaved. But
my grandfather is sleeping when we come
  to his bedside,
opens his eyes only to smile, turns so that
  my grandmother
can press ice cubes against his lips. She
  tells us,
He needs his rest now. That evening
he dies.

On the day he is buried, my sister and I
  wear white dresses,
the boys in white shirts and ties.
We walk slowly through Nicholtown, a long
  parade of people
who loved him — Hope, Dell, Roman and
  me
leading it. This is how we bury our dead —
  a silent parade
through the streets, showing the world our
  sadness, others
who knew my grandfather joining in on the
  walk,

children waving,
grown-ups dabbing at their eyes.

Ashes to ashes, we say at the grave site
with each handful of dirt we drop gently
  onto his lowering casket.
We will see you in the by and by, we say.
We will see you in the by and by.

HOW TO LISTEN #7

Even the silence
has a story to tell you.
Just listen. Listen.

PART V

ready
to change
the
world

AFTER GREENVILLE #2

After Daddy dies
my grandmother sells the house in
  Nicholtown
gives the brown chair to Miss Bell,
Daddy's clothes to the Brothers at the
  Kingdom Hall,
the kitchen table and bright yellow chairs
to her sister Lucinda in Fieldcrest Village.

After Daddy dies
my grandmother brings the bed our
  mother was born in
to Brooklyn. Unpacks her dresses
in the small empty bedroom
downstairs,
puts her Bible, *Watchtower*s and *Awake*s,
a picture of Daddy
on the little brown bookshelf.

After Daddy dies
spring blurs into summer

then winter comes on too cold and fast,
and my grandmother moves a chair to the
  living room
window
watches the tree drop the last of its leaves

while boys play skelly and spinning tops in
  the middle
of our quiet Brooklyn street.

After Daddy dies
I learn to jump double Dutch slowly
tripping again and again over my too-big
  feet. Counting,
Ten, twenty, thirty, forty deep into the winter
  until
one afternoon
gravity releases me and my feet fly free in
  the ropes,
fifty, sixty, seventy, eighty, ninety . . .

as my grandmother watches me.
Both of our worlds
changed forever.

MIMOSA TREE

A mimosa tree, green and thin limbed,
  pushes up through
the snow. My grandmother brought the
  seeds with her
from *back home.*

Sometimes, she pulls a chair to the
  window, looks
down over the yard.

The promise of glittering sidewalks feels a
  long time
behind us now, no diamonds anywhere to
  be found.

But some days, just after snow falls,
the sun comes out, shines down on the
  promise
of that tree from *back home* joining us
  here.

Shines down over the bright white ground.

And on those days, so much light and
   warmth fills
the room that it's hard not to believe
in a little bit

of everything.

BUBBLE-GUM CIGARETTES

You can buy a box of bubble-gum
  cigarettes for a dime
at the bodega around the corner.
Sometimes, Maria and I walk there,
our fingers laced together, a nickel
in each of our pockets.

The bubble gum is pink with white paper
wrapped around it. When you put it in
  your mouth
and blow, a white puff comes out.
You can really believe
you're smoking.

We talk with the bubble-gum cigarettes
between our fingers. Hold them in the air
like the movie stars on TV. We let them
  dangle
from our mouths and look at each other
through slitted eyes
then laugh at how grown-up we can be

how beautiful.

When my sister sees us
pretending to smoke, she shakes her head.
That's why Daddy died, she says.
After that
me and Maria peel the paper off,
turn our cigarettes into regular bubble
   gum.
After that
the game is over.

What's Left Behind

You've got your daddy's easy way,
my grandmother says to me, holding
the picture of my grandfather
in her hands. *I watch you with
your friends and see him all over again.*

> *Where will the wedding supper be?*
> *Way down yonder in a hollow tree . . .*

We look at the picture without talking.
Sometimes, I don't know the words for
  things,
how to write down the feeling of knowing
that every dying person leaves something
  behind.

I got my grandfather's easy way. Maybe
I know this when I'm laughing. Maybe
I know it when I think of Daddy
and he feels close enough
for me to lay my head against his shoulder.

I remember how he laughed, I tell my
  grandmother
and she smiles and says,

Because you laugh just like him.
Two peas in a pod, you were.

Two peas in a pod we were.

THE STORIES I TELL

Every autumn, the teacher asks us to
write about summer vacation
and read it to the class.

In Brooklyn, everybody goes south
or to Puerto Rico
or to their cousin's house in Queens.

But after my grandmother moves to New
York,
we only go down south once,
for my aunt Lucinda's funeral. After that,
my grandmother says she's done with the
South
says it makes her too sad.

But now
when summer comes

our family gets on a plane, flies
to

357

Africa
Hawaii
Chicago.

For summer vacation we went to Long
  Island,
to the beach. Everybody went fishing and
  everybody
caught a lot of fish.

Even though no one in my family has ever
  been
to Long Island
or fished
or likes the ocean — too deep, too scary.
  Still,
each autumn, I write a story.

In my writing, there is a stepfather now
who lives in California but meets us
  wherever we go.
There is a church, not a Kingdom Hall.
There is a blue car, a new dress, loose
  unribboned hair.

In my stories, our family is regular as air
two boys, two girls, sometimes a dog.

Did that really happen? the kids in class ask.

Yeah, I say. *If it didn't, how would I know what to write?*

How to Listen #8

Do you remember . . . ?
someone's always asking and
someone always does.

Fate & Faith & Reasons

Everything happens for a reason, my mother
says. Then tells me how Kay believed
in fate and destiny — everything
that ever happened or was going to happen
couldn't ever be avoided. The marchers
down south didn't just up and start
their marching — it was part of a longer,
  bigger
plan, that maybe belonged to God.

My mother tells me this as we fold
  laundry, white towels
separated from the colored ones. Each
a threat to the other and I remember the
  time
I spilled bleach on a blue towel, dotting it
  forever.
The pale pink towel, a memory
of when it was washed with a red one.
  Maybe
there is something, after all, to the way

some people want to remain — each to its
  own kind.
But in time
maybe
everything will fade to gray.

Even all of us coming to Brooklyn,
my mother says, *wasn't some accident.* And
  I can't help
thinking of the birds here — how they
  disappear
in the wintertime,
heading south for food and warmth and
  shelter.
Heading south
to stay alive . . . passing us on the way . . .

No accidents, my mother says. *Just fate and
  faith
and reasons.*

When I ask my mother what she believes
  in,
she stops, midfold, and looks out the back
  window.

Autumn

is full on here and the sky is bright blue.

I guess I believe in right now, she says. *And*

the resurrection.
And Brooklyn. And the four of you.

WHAT IF . . . ?

Maria's mother never left Bayamón, Puerto
    Rico,
and my mother never left Greenville.

What if no one had ever walked the grassy
    fields
that are now Madison Street and said,
Let's put some houses here.

What if the people in Maria's building
    didn't sell
1279 Madison Street
to Maria's parents
and our landlord told my mom that he
    couldn't rent
1283
to someone who already had four children.

What if the park with the swings wasn't
    right across
Knickerbocker Avenue?

What if Maria hadn't walked out of her
 building
one day and said,
My name is Maria but my mom calls me
 Googoo.
What if I had laughed instead of saying,

You're lucky. I wish I had a nickname, too.
You want to go to the park sometime?

What if she didn't have a sister and two
 brothers
and I didn't have a sister and two brothers
and her dad didn't teach us to box
and her mother didn't cook such good
 food?

I can't even imagine any of it, Maria says.

Nope, I say. *Neither can I.*

Bushwick History Lesson

Before German mothers wrapped scarves
    around
    their heads,
kissed their own mothers good-bye and
    headed across
    the world
to Bushwick —

Before the Italian fathers sailed across the
    ocean
for the dream of America
and found themselves in Bushwick —

Before Dominican daughters donned
    quinceañera
    dresses and walked proudly down
    Bushwick Avenue —

Before young brown boys in cutoff shorts
    spun their
    first tops and played their first games of

skelly on
Bushwick Streets —

Before any of that, this place was called
  Boswijck,

settled by the Dutch
and Franciscus the Negro, a former slave
who bought his freedom.

And all of New York was called New
  Amsterdam,
  run by a man
named Peter Stuyvesant. There were slaves
  here.
Those who could afford to own
their freedom
lived on the other side of the wall.
And now that place is called Wall Street.

When my teacher says, *So write down what
  all of this means
to you,* our heads bend over our notebooks,
  the whole class
silent. The whole class belonging
  somewhere:
Bushwick.

I didn't just appear one day.
I didn't just wake up and know how to write

my name.

I keep writing, knowing now
that I was a long time coming.

How to Listen #9

Under the back porch
there's an alone place I go
writing all I've heard.

THE PROMISE LAND

When my uncle gets out of jail
he isn't just my uncle anymore, he is
Robert the Muslim and wears
a small black *kufi* on his head.

And even though we know
we Witnesses are the chosen ones, we listen
to the stories he tells about
a man named Muhammad
and a holy place called Mecca
and the strength of all Black people.

We sit in a circle around him, his hands
moving slow through the air, his voice
calmer and quieter than it was before
he went away.

When he pulls out a small rug to pray on
I kneel beside him, wanting to see
his Mecca
wanting to know the place

he calls the Promise Land.

Look with your heart and your head, he tells
  me
his own head bowed.
It's out there in front of you.
You'll know when you get there.

POWER TO THE PEOPLE

On the TV screen a woman
named Angela Davis is telling us
there's a revolution going on and that it's
    time

for Black people to defend themselves.

So Maria and I walk through the streets,
our fists raised in the air Angela Davis
    style.

We read about her in the *Daily News,* run
to the television each time she's
    interviewed.

She is beautiful and powerful and has
my same gap-toothed smile. We dream
of running away to California
to join the Black Panthers
the organization Angela is a part of.

She is not afraid, she says,
to die for what she believes in
but doesn't plan to die
without a fight.

The FBI says Angela Davis is one of
  America's
Most Wanted.

Already, there are so many things I don't
  understand, why
someone would have to die
or even fight for what they believe in.

Why the cops would want someone who is
  trying
to change the world
in jail.

We are not afraid to die, Maria and I shout,
  fists high,
for what we believe in.
But both of us know — we'd rather keep
  believing
and live.

SAY IT LOUD

My mother tells us the Black Panthers are
  doing
all kinds of stuff
to make the world a better place for Black
  children.

In Oakland, they started a free breakfast
  program
so that poor kids can have a meal
before starting their school day. Pancakes,
toast, eggs, fruit: we watch the kids eat
  happily,
sing songs about how proud they are
to be Black. We sing the song along with
  them
stand on the bases of lampposts and
  scream,
Say it loud: I'm Black and I'm proud until
my mother hollers from the window,
Get down before you break your neck.

I don't understand the revolution.
In Bushwick, there's a street we can't cross called
Wyckoff Avenue. White people live on the other side.
Once a boy from my block got beat up for walking
over there.
Once there were four white families on our block
but they all moved away except for the old lady
who lives by the tree. Some days, she brings out cookies
tells us stories of the old neighborhood when everyone
was German or Irish and even some Italians
down by Wilson Avenue.
All kinds of people, she says. And the cookies
are too good for me to say,

Except us.

Everyone knows where they belong here.
It's not Greenville

but it's not diamond sidewalks either.

I still don't know what it is
that would make people want to get along.

Maybe no one does.

Angela Davis smiles, gap-toothed and
    beautiful,
    raises her fist in the air
says, *Power to the people,* looks out from
    the television

directly into my eyes.

MAYBE MECCA

There is a teenager on our block with one
   arm missing,
we call him Leftie and he tells us
he lost his arm in Vietnam.
That's a war, he says. *Y'all lucky to be too
   young to go.*
It doesn't hurt anymore, he tells us when we
   gather
around him.
But his eyes are sad eyes and some days he
   walks
around the block
maybe a hundred times without saying
   anything
to anyone.
When we call, *Hey Leftie!* he doesn't even
   look our way.

Some evenings, I kneel toward Mecca with
   my uncle.
Maybe Mecca

is the place Leftie goes to in his mind,
  when
the memory of losing
his arm becomes too much. Maybe Mecca
  is
good memories,
presents and stories and poetry and *arroz*
  con pollo
and family and friends . . .

Maybe Mecca is the place everyone is
  looking for . . .

It's out there in front of you, my uncle says.

I know I'll know it
when I get there.

THE REVOLUTION

Don't wait for your school to teach you, my
  uncle says,
about the revolution. It's happening in the
  streets.

He's been out of jail for more than a year
  now and his hair
is an afro again, gently moving in the wind
  as we head
to the park, him holding tight
to my hand even when we're not crossing
Knickerbocker Avenue, even now when I'm
  too old
for hand holding *and the like.*

The revolution is when Shirley Chisholm
  ran for president
and the rest of the world tried to imagine
a Black woman in the White House.

When I hear the word

revolution
I think of the carousel with
all those beautiful horses
going around as though they'll never stop
  and me
choosing the purple one each time,
  climbing up onto it
and reaching for the golden ring, as soft
  music plays.

*The revolution is always going to be
  happening.*

I want to write this down, that the
  revolution is like
a merry-go-round, history always being
  made
somewhere. And maybe for a short time,
we're a part of that history. And then the
  ride stops
and our turn is over.

We walk slow toward the park where I can
  already see
the big swings, empty and waiting for me.

And after I write it down, maybe I'll end it
  this way:

My name is Jacqueline Woodson
and I am ready for the ride.

How to Listen #10

Write down what I think
I know. The knowing will come.

Just keep listening . . .

A Writer

You're a writer, Ms. Vivo says,
her gray eyes bright behind
thin wire frames. Her smile bigger than
    anything
so I smile back, happy to hear these words
from a teacher's mouth. She is a feminist,
    she tells us
and thirty fifth-grade hands bend into
    desks
where our dictionaries wait to open yet
    another
world to us. Ms. Vivo pauses, watches our
    fingers fly
Webster's has our answers.
Equal rights, a boy named Andrew yells
    out.
For women.
My hands freeze on the thin white pages.
Like Blacks, Ms. Vivo, too, is part of a
    revolution.

But right now, that revolution is so far
   away from me.
This moment, this *here,* this *right now* is
   my teacher
   saying,
You're a writer, as she holds the poem I am
   just beginning.
The first four lines, stolen
from my sister:

*Black brothers, Black sisters, all of them
   were great
no fear no fright but a willingness to fight . . .*

You can have them, Dell said when she
   saw.
I don't want to be a poet.

And then my own pencil moving late into
   the evening:

*In big fine houses lived the whites
in little old shacks lived the blacks
but the blacks were smart
in fear they took no part.
One of them was Martin
with a heart of gold.*

You're a writer, Ms. Vivo says, holding my
   poem out to me.

And standing in front of the class
taking my poem from her
my voice shakes as I recite the first line:

Black brothers, Black sisters, all of them
  were great. . . .

But my voice grows stronger with each
  word because
more than anything else in the world,
I want to believe her.

Every Wish, One Dream

Every dandelion blown
each *Star light, star bright,*
The first star I see tonight.

My wish is always the same.

Every fallen eyelash
and first firefly of summer . . .

The dream remains.

What did you wish for?
To be a writer.

Every heads-up penny found
and daydream and night dream
and even when people say it's a pipe
  dream . . . !

I want to be a writer.

Every sunrise and sunset and song

against a cold windowpane.

Passing the mountains.

Passing the sea.

Every story read
every poem remembered:

I loved my friend
and
When I see birches bend to left and right
and
"Nay," answered the child: "but these are the
   wounds of Love."

Every memory . . .

Froggie went a-courting, and he did ride
Uh hmm.

brings me closer
and closer to the dream.

THE EARTH FROM FAR AWAY

Every Saturday morning, we run downstairs
to the television. Just as the theme song
from *The Big Blue Marble* begins, the four
  of us sing along:

*The earth's a big blue marble when you see
it from out there.*

Then the camera is zooming in on that
  marble,
  the blue becoming
water, then land, then children in Africa
  and Texas
  and China
and Spain and sometimes, New York City!
  The world
close enough to touch now and children
  from all over
right in our living room! Telling us their
  stories.

The sun and moon declare, our beauty's very rare . . .

The world — *my* world! — like words.
   Once
there was only the letter *J* and my sister's
   hand
wrapped around mine, guiding me,
   promising me
infinity. This big blue marble
of world and words and people and places

inside my head and

somewhere out there, too.

All of it, mine now if I just listen

and write it down.

WHAT I BELIEVE

I believe in God and evolution.
I believe in the Bible and the Qur'an.
I believe in Christmas and the New World.
I believe that there is good in each of us
no matter who we are or what we believe
  in.
I believe in the words of my grandfather.
I believe in the city and the South
the past and the present.
I believe in Black people and White people
  coming together.
I believe in nonviolence and "Power to the
  People."
I believe in my little brother's pale skin and
  my own dark brown.
I believe in my sister's brilliance and the
  too-easy books I love to read.
I believe in my mother on a bus and Black
  people refusing to ride.
I believe in good friends and good food.

I believe in johnny pumps and jump ropes,
Malcolm and Martin, Buckeyes and
  Birmingham,
writing and listening, bad words and good
  words —
I believe in Brooklyn!

I believe in one day and someday and this
  perfect moment called *Now.*

EACH WORLD

When there are many worlds
you can choose the one
you walk into each day.

You can imagine yourself brilliant as your
  sister,
slower moving, quiet and thoughtful as
  your older brother
or filled up with the hiccupping joy and
  laughter
of the baby in the family.

You can imagine yourself a mother now,
  climbing
onto a bus at nightfall, turning
to wave good-bye to your children,
  watching
the world of South Carolina disappear
  behind you.

When there are many worlds, love can

wrap itself
around you, say, *Don't cry.* Say, *You are as
 good as anyone.*
Say, *Keep remembering me.* And you know,
 even as the world explodes
around you — that you are loved . . .

Each day a new world
opens itself up to you. And all the worlds
 you are —

Ohio and Greenville
Woodson and Irby
Gunnar's child and Jack's daughter
Jehovah's Witness and nonbeliever
listener and writer
Jackie and Jacqueline —

gather into one world

called You

where You decide

what each world
and each story
and each ending

will finally be.

AUTHOR'S NOTE

Memory is strange. When I first began to write *Brown Girl Dreaming,* my childhood memories of Greenville came flooding back to me — small moments and bigger ones, too. Things I hadn't thought about in years and other stuff I've never forgotten. When I began to write it all down, I realized how much I missed the South. So for the first time in many years, I returned "home," and saw cousins I hadn't seen since I was small, heard stories I had heard many times from my grandmother, walked roads that were very different now but still the same roads of my childhood. It was a bittersweet journey. I wish I could have walked those roads again with my mom, my grandfather, my uncle Robert, my aunt Kay, and my grandmother. But all have made their own journey to the next place. So I walked the roads alone this time. Still, it felt as though each of them was with me — they're all deeply etched now, into memory.

And that's what this book is — my past, my people, my memories, my story.

I knew I couldn't write about the South without writing about Ohio. And even though I was only a baby when we lived there, I have the gift of my amazing aunt Ada Adams, who is a genealogist and our family historian. She was my go-to person and filled in so many gaps in my memory. Aunt Ada took me right back to Columbus. During the writing of this book, I returned to Ohio with my family. Aunt Ada took us on a journey of the Underground Railroad, showed us the graves of grandparents and great-grandparents, told me so much history I had missed out on as a child. Aunt Ada not only showed me the past but she also helped me understand the present. So often, I am asked where my stories come from. I know now my stories are part of a continuum — my aunt is a storyteller. So were my mom and my grandmother. And the history Aunt Ada showed me — the rich history that is *my* history — made me at once proud and thoughtful. The people who came before me worked so hard to make this world a better place for me. I know my work is to make the world a better place for those coming after. As long as I can remember this, I can continue to do the work I was put here to do.

On the journey to writing this book, my dad, Jack Woodson, chimed in when he could. Even as I write this, I smile because my father always makes me laugh. I like to think I acquired a bit of his sense of humor. I didn't know him for many years. When I met him again at the age of fourteen, it was as though a puzzle piece had dropped from the air and landed right where it belonged. My dad is that puzzle piece.

Gaps were also filled in by my friend Maria, who helped the journey along with pictures and stories. When we were little, we used to say we'd one day be old ladies together, sitting in rocking chairs remembering our childhood and laughing. We've been friends for nearly five decades now and still call each other My Forever Friend. I hope everyone has a Forever Friend in their life.

But at the end of the day, I was alone with *Brown Girl Dreaming* — walking through these memories and making sense out of myself as a writer in a way I had never done before.

I am often asked if I had a hard life growing up. I think my life was very complicated and very rich. Looking back on it, I think my life was at once ordinary and amazing. I couldn't imagine any other life. I know that I was lucky enough to be born during a time when the world was changing like crazy — and that I was a part of that change. I know that I was and continue to be loved. I couldn't ask for anything more.

THANKFULS

I am thankful for my memory. When it needed help on the journey, I am also thankful for my fabulous editor, Nancy Paulsen. More help came from Sara LaFleur. This book wouldn't be in the world without my family, including Hope, Odella, and Roman, Toshi, Jackson-Leroi, and Juliet — thank you for your patience and thorough reading and rereading. Thanks to my forever friend, Maria Cortez-Ocasio, her husband, Sam, and her daughters Jillian, Samantha, and Angelina. Even her grandson, Little Sammy. And of course, her mom, Darma — thanks for feeding me so well over the years.

Toshi Reagon, thanks for reading this and sitting with me as I fretted over it. Thanks for your music, your guidance, your stories.

On the Ohio side: a big big thank-you to my aunt Ada — genealogist extraordinaire! — and to my aunt Alicia and my uncle David and, of course, my dad, Jack Woodson.

On the Greenville side: big thanks to my cousins Michael and Sheryl Irby, Megan Irby, Michael and Kenneth Sullivan, Dorothy Vaughn-Welch, Samuel Miller, La'Brandon, Monica Vaughn, and all my other relatives who opened their doors, let me in, told me their stories!

In North Carolina, thanks so much to Stephanie Grant, Ara Wilson, Augusta, and Josephine for that fabulously quiet guest room and dinner at the end of the day for many days until this book was close to being in the world.

On the Brooklyn and Vermont sides: thanks to my village. So grateful for all of you!

In memory: thanks to my mom, Mary Anne Woodson, my uncles Odell and Robert Irby, my grandmother Georgiana Scott Irby, my grandfather Gunnar Irby, and my aunt Hallique Caroline (Kay) Irby.

These thankfuls wouldn't be complete without acknowledging the myriad teachers who, in many different ways, pointed this brown girl toward her dream.

jacqueline
as a child

jacqueline's parents

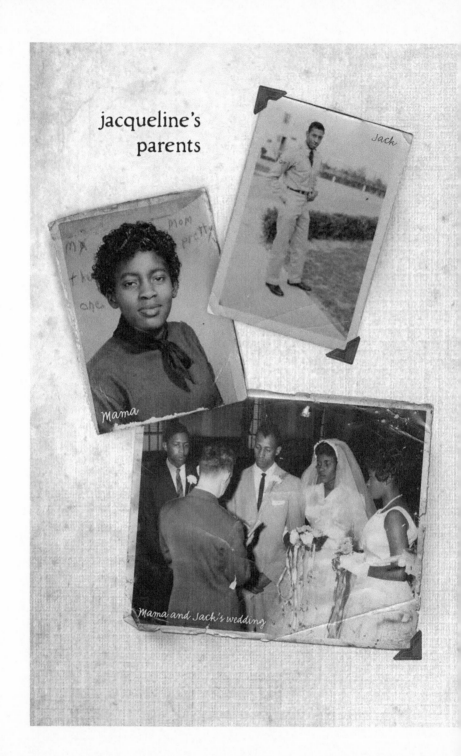

Jack

Mama

Mama and Jack's wedding

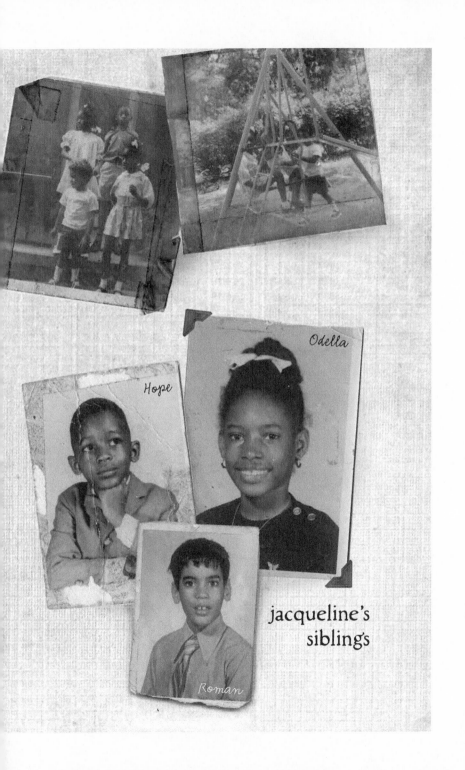

Hope

Odella

Roman

jacqueline's
siblings

the woodsons of ohio

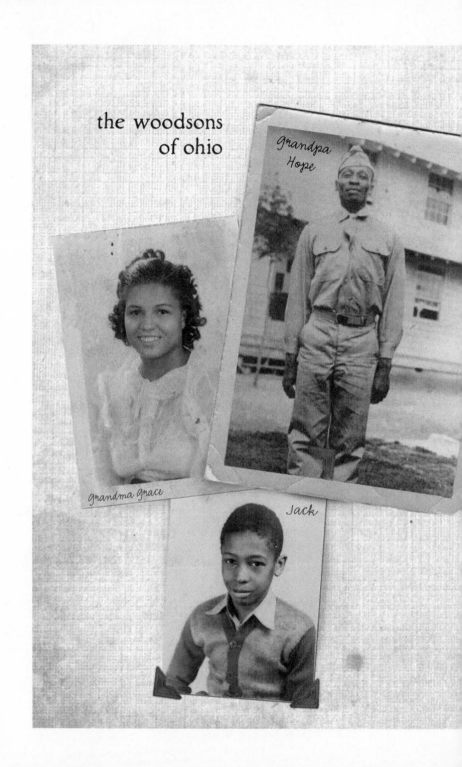

grandpa Hope

grandma grace

Jack

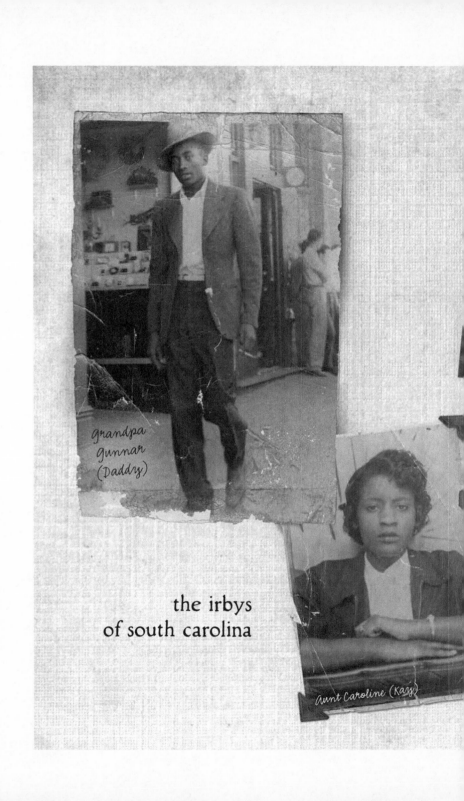

grandpa
gunnar
(Daddy)

the irbys
of south carolina

aunt Caroline (Kass)

Grandma Georgiana

Mama

Uncle Odell

Uncle Robert

ABOUT THE AUTHOR

Jacqueline Woodson (www.jacqueline woodson.com) is the 2014 National Book Award Winner for her *New York Times* bestselling memoir *Brown Girl Dreaming,* which was also a recipient of the Coretta Scott King Award, a Newbery Honor Award, the NAACP Image Award and the Sibert Honor Award. Woodson was recently named the Young People's Poet Laureate by the Poetry Foundation. She is the author of more than two dozen award-winning books for young adults, middle graders and children; among her many accolades, she is a four-time Newbery Honor winner, a three-time National Book Award finalist, and a two-time Coretta Scott King Award winner. Her books include *The Other Side, Each Kindness,* the Caldecott Honor Book *Coming on Home Soon;* the Newbery Honor winners *Feathers, Show Way,* and *After Tu-*

pac and D Foster, and *Miracle's Boys* which received the *LA Times* Book Prize and the Coretta Scott King Award and was adapted into a miniseries directed by Spike Lee. Jacqueline is also the recipient of the Margaret A. Edwards Award for lifetime achievement for her contributions to young adult literature, the winner of the Jane Addams Children's Book Award, the 2013 United States nominee for the Hans Christian Andersen Award, and a 2016 National Book Award finalist for her adult novel *Another Brooklyn.* She lives with her family in Brooklyn, New York.

The employees of Thorndike Press hope you have enjoyed this Large Print book. All our Thorndike, Wheeler, and Kennebec Large Print titles are designed for easy reading, and all our books are made to last. Other Thorndike Press Large Print books are available at your library, through selected bookstores, or directly from us.

For information about titles, please call:
(800) 223-1244

or visit our website at:
gale.com/thorndike

To share your comments, please write:
Publisher
Thorndike Press
10 Water St., Suite 310
Waterville, ME 04901